CL

Changing Impressions

CLASS OF '88

2

Changing Impressions

Linda A. Cooney

ARMADA

First published in USA by Scholastic Inc. in 1987
First published in UK by Armada in 1988

Armada is an imprint of
the Children's Division, part of
the Collins Publishing Group,
8 Grafton Street, London W1X 3LA

Copyright © 1987 by Linda Alper and Kevin Cooney

Printed and bound in Great Britain by
William Collins Sons & Co. Ltd, Glasgow

Changing Impressions

CHAPTER
1

Celia had her eye on him. Past the counter of the Chili Place where she worked, down the Redwood Mall corridor, right next to the huge tree that still twinkled even though it was two days after Christmas; there he was.

He was handsome, too — dark blond hair, great eyes, sunglasses hanging around his neck (Vuarnets no doubt), and a red sweater with a leaping reindeer. She could see that he had suntan marks from a Christmas skiing vacation, and he was probably a junior or senior, since a set of car keys was dangling conspicuously from his left hand.

Now he turned and looked at her again, but she didn't show anything other than a tiny smile. That was part of it. Stay cool, pretend you're smiling at the shoppers or a friend in the shoe store or looking at the white-flocked window of the Benetton's, while all the time you're oh-so-aware of him.

It was a game they were playing — the flirtation game — and Celia had played it a million times before. She would do her best to act like she hadn't noticed him, and he would do his best to act the same way right back. It was a little embarrassing since she was on duty: The uniform Celia had on was supremely dumb, a lime green smock with a white cardboard visor. Good thing Celia knew she had looks — wavy blonde hair, peachy skin, blue green eyes — because the uniform made her feel about as attractive as a stray chili bean. But that was what you put up with when you worked a fast-food counter; none of the girls behind any other counter looked any better. Celia knew it. If they did, he'd be hanging around the Muffin Man, the Croissant Corner, or the Coffee Klatch. No, it was chili burgers for this guy; chili burgers all the way.

As if to confirm it, Celia looked up and saw that he was walking right toward her. She quickly began swabbing the counter.

"Hi."

"Oh." She tried to sound surprised. "Hi."

Then he really did surprise her. He hiked himself up and plopped down on the middle of the stainless steel counter. Pat, Celia's boss, would have a fit if he saw it. That realization made her feel charged, giggly, although she didn't let herself laugh.

"Did I say you could sit there?" she challenged.

"Did I ask? Besides, I could tell you wanted me to."

2

"Oh, really? If I wanted you to jump into that pot of chili, would you do that, too?"

"You wouldn't want me to do that, would you?"

"Don't tempt me."

Ooooh, I've gotten good at this, Celia thought, really enjoying the game. She put both elbows down on the counter and cradled her face to look at him. Flirting came naturally to her, the way some girls had perfect pitch or could do splits. Celia knew it was a good thing, otherwise guys wouldn't notice her at all. She didn't have rich parents or a nice car or a beautiful house to help her. All she had were her looks and her smarts.

"What's your name?" the boy persisted, leaning — then practically lying — on her chili counter.

"What's yours?"

"I asked you first."

"Doesn't mean I'm going to tell you."

She'd gotten to him again, she could tell. It was great, and Celia felt a little tingle. She was good at this because she'd had so much practice. All sophomore year, the mall had been her social life. It had taken the place of football games and dances and Redwood High spirit rallies, which she hadn't attended since last year, when she was a freshman. Not counting Meg, Allie, her cousin Nick, and Sean — Celia's best and oldest friends in the entire world — Redwood High social life had soured for her. That was one of the reasons she hadn't minded spending every weekend since last summer at the mall.

3

Celia raised her eyes, finally looking at the boy. Then she drew a lazy circle on the metal counter. "Do you go to Redwood High?" She'd never seen him in class or in the halls, and this was certainly a boy she'd remember.

"Do you?"

"Guess."

"I'd guess you do. Am I right?"

"Maybe. What about you?"

"Fair's fair. You guess."

Celia put a finger to her lips. "I'd guess that you live in San Francisco and are only in Redwood Hills to visit your poor sick grandmother." Redwood Hills was a medium-sized rural town over an hour north of the city — nowhere near as sophisticated as San Francisco — so Celia was laying on the flattery. That was another thing she'd learned. Let them think they're getting somewhere, then pull the rug out when they least expect it.

"Close," he admitted with a cocky nod. "What year are you? Junior?"

Now she suspected it was he who was doing the flattering. Surely he could tell that she was only a sophomore. "Are you?"

"Do you always answer a question with a question?"

"Do you?"

"Only when I really want to know something."

"What is it you want to know?"

"Everything about you."

His eyes shone with confidence, and he bumped her with his elbow. She was already thinking ahead, figuring out her comeback to the next inevitable questions — When do you get off work? And, What's your telephone number? Not that she didn't date, but even with a guy as gorgeous as this one, the initial flirtation was the most exciting part. After that Celia just felt restless, unsure, and a little scared. Besides, it was better if a guy like this didn't know too much about her.

The perfect comeback was gelling when she heard a low, husky voice that made her thoughts go haywire. She was praying it wasn't, it couldn't be, when the husky voice got louder, and she saw the petite body that went with it, buried under a mountain of packages, storming out of Nordstrom's department store.

"CHRISTOPHER! Christopher, did you find me a Coke?" Whitney Hain was yelling down the mall. She was all in leather, like some wild animal, dark hair flying, her smoky voice filled with irritation.

The boy hopped off the counter as if it were a hot stove and guiltily slipped on his Vuarnets. Obviously, he was Christopher. He shot Celia a tiny, secret smile as Whitney raced up to join him. Then he started to lead Whitney over to the Muffin Man and dropped his arm over her shoulder.

"I'm dying of thirst," Whitney panted, handing her packages to Christopher and not noticing Celia. "I should have known not to try and exchange things today. Every lowlife in town is here for the sales."

Just looking at Whitney still made Celia curdle inside. Whitney was one of the main reasons that the social scene at Redwood High no longer appealed to her. Freshman year, Celia had been on top of the world: A cheerleader, and for a short time, one of the many Whitney Hain followers. But Whitney had been nasty to Celia's good friends Allie and Sean, so Celia had finally told her off. Actually Whitney had been pretty condescending to Celia, too.

Whitney unzipped her leather jacket, which was creamy beige, like her complexion. She stood with her hand on her hip as if she were modeling the matching jacket and pants — surely a Christmas present — and something that Celia couldn't afford if she dished up chili for the rest of her life. Whitney made a pout with her rosebud mouth, fluttered her hand to shake down three gold bracelets, and sighed. It was somewhere in the middle of that sigh that she noticed Celia.

"Oh, hello," Whitney stated coldly as she pulled away from Christopher and stood taut. She looked Celia up and down, then smirked at her Chili Place uniform.

"Hi, Whitney." Celia tried to appear unruffled. She gave a phony, sweet smile. "Want a chili dog?"

"Spare me," Whitney came back instantly. "I forgot you worked here." Whitney's steel gray eyes were now examining the food booth as if it were selling dead rats. "Nice." Whitney's voice dripped sarcasm.

Celia stared back with all the toughness she

6

could muster. Her heart was rapping like an angry snaredrum, but she was determined to act cool.

"Just give us two Cokes," Whitney ordered.

"Yes, your highness," Celia shot back.

Whitney gave Celia one of her "You are nothing" looks. It was the look she'd given Celia all freshman year after Celia'd told her off. They were both still Cheerleaders, and Celia had to see her every week at basketball games and track meets. It was no wonder that after freshman year, Celia had vowed never to go to another Redwood sporting event as long as she lived.

Celia put two Cokes on the counter. Whitney pushed her cup back to Celia. "More ice."

Celia glared.

"Please," Whitney begged in a phony little-girl voice.

Celia gritted her teeth and opened the ice bin. All she needed was Whitney at her counter treating her like a personal maid. Celia prided herself on having gotten the better of Whitney freshman year; and yet Whitney was still a cheerleader and still wore great clothes and led a crowd of wealthy, popular girls at Redwood High while Celia stood in the mall, sweating and fetching her extra ice. Maybe that was why Celia sometimes felt insecure about who had really won the final victory.

"Celia, Christopher needs more ice, too."

Celia was considering taking her scoop full of ice and flinging it right in Whitney's beautiful face, but she heard her boss, Pat, puttering around in back, and controlled herself. She dropped three cubes into Christopher's Coke and tried to think of a way to keep Whitney from winning this round. It didn't take Celia long. As she took Whitney's money to the register, she smiled back over her shoulder at Christopher.

"Christopher!" Celia said with mock surprise. "So that's his name! He was so busy asking me questions that he didn't have time to tell me. He sure wanted to know my name." She came back to the counter and patted Whitney's shoulder. Whitney flinched. "Don't worry, I didn't tell him."

Christopher's cool posture stiffened. Whitney whipped around accusingly to face him. Celia was on the right track. He was clearly Whitney's new boyfriend, and Whitney was ripe for jealousy. He slipped off his glasses and was flashing Celia angry cool-it looks. Celia continued. "I was just standing here, minding my own business, just tending my poor little pot of chili, when he came up and sat on my counter and said he wanted to know everything about me."

Whitney's pale skin was beginning to look sunburned as she grimaced at Christopher. He put his hands on her slim arms and tried to soothe her. "She's making it up, Whit," he said in a syrupy tone.

For one second Whitney allowed her anger to show. She jerked her arm away. "You creep," she accused her boyfriend. "You flirt with every girl you see. Even a lowlife like her." She stomped her foot. "Maybe you should go behind the counter and make chili together." Her voice had turned to a dusky whine. "Oh, Christopher. I can't believe you'd pay attention to *her*."

Celia smiled smugly.

"What are you smiling about?" Whitney demanded. "You're hardly Christopher's type. It figures you'd pick him up in the mall. He'd stay interested in you for about ten seconds. Gee, maybe you could invite him over to your lovely house, and introduce him to your mother. Maybe he'd want to go out with her, too."

Celia cringed, embarrassed, and tried to hide a crusty orange blotch she'd just noticed on her sleeve. Why did Whitney always have to play so dirty? Celia's single mom worked as a hairdresser downtown and often looked outrageous — a pink streak in her hair, glittery stockings, and short skirts, anything weird or way out. And she and Celia lived in a small, run-down rented house near downtown. But big deal. Just because Whitney's parents had one of the largest wineries in Northern California and owned half of Redwood Hills. . . . It made Celia furious.

Christopher kissed Whitney on the forehead, still trying to placate her. "Cool it, Whit. She's not the kind of girl you take seriously. I was just playing with her." Whitney's pout stayed firm. He lightly slapped her shoulder. "Come on, don't be a jerk." He started down the mall, anxious to get away. "I'm going to see what's in the video store. You coming?"

"In a sec." Whitney watched him go but lingered at the counter. Finally she turned back to Celia. "I don't know why I got so upset," she said with a deep sigh. "He's right."

"About what?"

"You. Christopher goes to Birmingham prep school. He's very smart. And no guy like that is ever going to take you seriously."

Celia fought the rage that was starting to burn inside her. She was not going to let Whitney see just how deeply she was getting to her. "Oh, really. Who *does* he take seriously — Princess Diana?"

"Face it, Celia." The angry color in Whitney's face was gone. She was once again her normal, pale, composed self. Celia wasn't sure when or how Whitney had regained the upper hand. "You hang out with that nerdy brain, Sean Pendleton — what a joke he is — and the only reason Nick Rhodes isn't embarrassed to be seen with you is that you're his cousin. No decent guy has ever gone for you, and no one ever will."

Celia was struck speechless. Plenty of guys at Redwood had been nuts about her. It was just that she always lost interest once it went past the flirting stage. But she knew what Whitney meant. Special guys. Guys who went to prep school or were star quarterback or the son of someone rich and famous. Guys who could have any girl they wanted. Guys who were probably as phony as Christopher. "Do me a favor, Whitney. Don't worry about me and boys — decent or otherwise."

"Believe me. I won't. As far as I'm concerned, you're not worth thinking about at all." Whitney downed the last of her Coke, handed the empty cup to Celia, and marched off to join Christopher.

"Ugh," Celia moaned to herself as she watched Whitney go. The anger inside her was spreading

10

like a forest fire. She was boiling, overflowing with it. She threw Whitney's cup on the floor and pounded the counter with her fist.

She wasn't sure how it happened, but somehow Whitney had just scored another victory.

CHAPTER
2

Only three blocks away from the Redwood Mall, Nick Rhodes' mint green VW Rabbit (a hand-me-down from his oldest brother, but washed, shined, and waxed as if it were brand-new) was stopped at a traffic light.

"Hey, Nick, ten points for the lady crossing the street with the shopping bags."

"Sean!" Allie let out her loud, goofy laugh and pitched forward against the Rabbit's front seat. "Twenty points for the car with the 'Baby on Board' sticker." She fell back against her boyfriend, L.P., who was laughing, too.

Meg, who sat in the front next to Nick, turned back to them and made a face. "You guys are sick." She smiled devilishly. "Fifty points for ramming that police car!"

Nick shook his head. "You're all animals." He looked in the rearview mirror and talked to the reflection of Sean, Allie, and L.P. in the backseat. "Just keep cool and leave everything to the master."

There was a collective "Hmmm" and then, for at least thirty seconds, they all sat still and quiet. Nick was the first of them to turn sixteen and get his license — not counting L.P., who was a junior — so when the light changed and Nick calmly drove ahead, they all watched with admiration.

Meg was always amazed at the grace and ease with which Nick handled most everything. He coordinated the gearshift as surely as he ran down the football field or dribbled a basketball, and he commanded their admiration as effortlessly as he did the guys' on his team at school. Needless to say, lots of girls were crazy about him, too. They couldn't help staring at his green eyes and wide shoulders and blond hair — which was now shimmering from the shaft of winter sun pouring in his window. Meg didn't realize that she was staring, too, until Nick turned to face her and smiled. It was a warm, almost intimate, smile, one that couldn't help but remind her of how she'd once felt about him. But that was over. . . . She'd decided she and Nick were just pals. Feeling sure of that, she grabbed one of his packages from the floor and opened it.

"Hey, these are nice, Nick. Why are you returning them?" She held up a pair of pajamas designed like a baseball uniform, complete with feet and a hat that said SLUGGER. The backseat exploded with laughter.

"Oooh, Nick," Sean sang.

Allie howled, practically rocking the car with her famous high-pitched giggle. It was the kind of laugh that could crack up an entire movie theater. "Hey, Slugger!"

Even L.P. leaned forward and scratched his head, making his slightly punk hair stand straight up. "Gee, Nick, those are, uh . . . really different."

Nick whipped the pajamas out of Meg's hand and turned around, embarrassed, but laughing, too. "Yeah, well. Good old Aunt Effie. I think the last ten years have passed her by. Last Christmas she gave me a Snoopy lunch box."

"Maybe you should wear them to school on the same day," Meg taunted.

"Yeah." Allie giggled. "You could be the new sophomore mascot."

The light changed and Nick turned back. "Maybe I will. Now quiet down back there," he snapped in a mock growl, "I'm trying to drive."

They hushed as he drove past the tall trees and the jungle gyms and the bronze grizzly bear statue in Portola Park. It was cold enough to need the car heater, but the sun was so bright they all squinted when Nick made a left turn. He pulled into the tunnel leading to the mall's underground parking structure, where the winter light was replaced by fluorescent glow and car exhaust.

"What about you, Meg?" Allie asked, leaning against the front seat. As she did, her black bowler hat — a Christmas present from Celia — fell off her head, exposing her recently permed brown hair. It was clipped short on one side, and tumbled down, long and curly on the other. Allie's look, while always wild, changed frequently, and sophomore year she'd been into a

14

sort of early Pat Benatar mixed with Molly Ringwald.

"Yeah," Nick threw in. "How come you don't have anything to return?"

Meg tossed back her braid and shrugged. "I got what I wanted."

"Sure," giggled Allie. "More sweat shirts."

"A new organizer date book."

"Track shorts."

"Maybe something radical like black jeans instead of blue."

Meg ignored their teasing, leaned back, and held up her foot. She was wearing a brand-new pair of pink hightops with her Levi's, sweat shirt, and blazer. She had the most consistent fashion taste at Redwood, although even Allie had to admit that with Meg's long dark hair, lanky runner's build, and clear blue eyes, jeans and sweat shirts looked great on her. "What do you think of these?"

"Pink! Oooh."

Allie held on to Meg's shoe until Meg swung her leg away to look at the long line of cars waiting to pull into the lot. Nick leaned one arm on the steering wheel and looked back. "So what's the plan, everybody?"

"I'm going to Greenberg's photo store," said L.P.

"I have to go to Radio Shack," added Sean.

"I'm meeting Celia first thing," volunteered Meg.

"Good," Sean agreed. He was squeezed in the corner of the backseat and kept shifting, hoping to find a place for his long legs. He'd gotten so much taller in the last year that Meg's mother said she could see him grow before her very eyes. Finally finding a comfortable position, he stacked on his lap a computer chess game, a small robot, two new wave albums, and a bicycle racing shirt that was almost the exact color of his unruly red hair. He hadn't decided yet which of his gifts were keepers. "You definitely have to rescue Celia from the Chili Pit."

"Really."

"The Chili Pit?" wondered L.P. "I thought it was called the Chili Place."

"We think the Chili Pit is a more accurate description," Nick said. He smiled at Meg again and bumped her shoulder. "Right?"

Meg let her eyes linger on Nick's for an extra second. He gave her that look again. Meg was used to palling around with Nick, having him tickle her and tease her and generally drive her crazy. But she'd learned not to misinterpret the way he acted toward her and not to worry about it too much.

"I think Sean came up with the Chili Pit."

Sean nodded and tipped a finger to his forehead.

"I don't know," L.P. shrugged, absorbed with the new camera lens he had been holding. "Sounds about right to me." He slid his arm around Allie, pulling her against him. Sean moved even further into the corner, his freckled face reddening just a little.

Meg smiled as she watched L.P. and Allie. They looked so secure together, so right. L.P.

never even minded the times the rest of them used their own private jokes and pet names as if everyone else in the world understood them. She, Nick, Celia, Allie, and Sean had grown up together, so they had an endless supply of expressions that had been made up along the way. Even though Allie and L.P. had been together for over a year, there were tons of times when the group's private lingo went right past him. But L.P. never seemed to mind. Meg thought he was too secure in himself and in Allie's feelings for him to feel left out.

"But the big question is . . ." Nick started, then stopped as he finally pulled into the parking lot. Hundreds of cars were crawling up and down the aisles, and it looked as if there weren't a single empty space. ". . . What do we need for my New Year's Eve party?"

"Funny hats."

"Noisemakers."

"Streamers."

"Elephants!"

Nick pounded the steering wheel. "Dancing girls!"

Meg and Allie yelled at the same time, "Dancing boys!!"

Planning for this event had been going on for over a month. At first they weren't sure who should have the party, but Celia's house was way too small, Allie's mom and dad said no because of her baby sister, Sean's parents were too busy with holiday business in their bicycle store, and the same went for Meg's folks and their plant nursery. So Nick was the one. Besides, Nick's house was by far the biggest, and since his dad was a state senator, his mom was used to parties. It was a good thing, too, since Nick had invited over fifty kids.

"I'm doing all the stuff with the stereo," Sean announced. They were still inching up and down the parking aisles. There was a space halfway down the row, but the car in front of them grabbed it.

"L.P. and I'll decorate," said Allie.

Nick looked at Meg again, his green eyes glowing with warmth. "McCall, why don't you organize, especially the food. You're the best at that."

"Gee, thanks, Nick," she answered sarcastically. It figured that Nick would assume she'd want to organize it all. That had been her role since about seventh grade: Meg McCall — leader . . . organizer . . . responsible cookie-baker and do-gooder. Yuck. She was so sick of being a do-gooder, she wanted to scream.

"You and Celia could make those weird cheese things," Nick continued excitedly, "and those two-tone brownies you made for the sophomore bake sale."

"I'm honored."

Nick still didn't pick up on her sarcasm. It was just like at school this year. After working her brains out freshman year as class president, she'd decided no more class offices sophomore year. No more giving her life to her school. Let somebody else sweat and slave for a change. Then, come election time, she'd won as class treasurer by write-in vote. She hadn't even wanted to run, and she still got roped into it! After that, she'd ended up making brownies for the sophomore fundraiser, decorating the Thanksgiving dance, and running the entire Christmas canned food drive.

Meg was about to tell Nick exactly what he could do with her cookies and her cheese puffs, when Allie started hooting in the backseat, flapping her hands, and pointing. "Look!! NICK! A space! A space!!"

Sure enough there was an empty parking space, and Nick was about to drive right by it.

Nick slammed on the brakes, then made a sharp turn, just missing the next parked car. Meg was jolted against the window, and the next thing she knew she was hurling into Nick, her face against his shoulder, her hand trying to steady herself, grabbing his arm. He quickly pulled up the parking brake between them, faced her — his mouth only a few inches away, his eyes gazing into hers. He whispered, "Hi."

Meg's heart was in her mouth, and she could have killed him. He looked so relaxed, so innocent, she knew he felt none of the crashing and pounding that had started inside her. As fast as she could regain her balance, she hoisted herself against her door and climbed out.

Sean followed her, balancing his boxes and records, while L.P. and Allie got out on the other side. Doors slammed, the garage echoed with car horns and voices. Meg was waiting for her heart rate to return to normal, when she felt two warm hands tickling her side. Strong arms followed, and she gave a sharp jab with her elbow, plowing Nick in his middle and sending

him back against the car. But he just came at her
again, laughing this time, and twisting her arm
behind her back.

"You think you're so tough, McCall."

"Oh, yeah?"

"Yeah. So are you going to help with my
party or not?"

"Why should I?"

"Because the rest of us are too inept to do it
alone."

Now Meg started laughing, too. It was hard
for her to stay mad at Nick for too long. "That's
the worst excuse I've ever heard."

"Have you ever tasted my cooking?"

They were face to face now, daring each
other. "Practice. You'll get better."

"Show me how."

"Nick, just read a recipe. You don't need me."

"Oh, but I do need you, Meg." Before things
could get too out of hand, Nick had pulled Sean
over and had his arm around him. They were
almost the same height, although Sean was much
skinnier. "Don't we need her?"

Sean nodded, then pulled Allie over, too. L.P.
followed close behind. "We do. We all need you,
Meg!" they chanted together.

Meg put her hands on her hips and shook her
head. *"All right, I'll help!"* she yelled to the steel
rafters and the concrete floors. About a dozen
shoppers turned to stare.

"I knew you'd never let us down," Nick said,
leading the way toward the elevator.

"I bet you did," Meg grumbled under her
breath, watching his back. "I just bet you did."

CHAPTER 3

An hour later, Meg and Celia were in Marvin's Pet Store.

"Should I really quit?"

"Definitely."

"Right now?"

"There's no better time."

"I sure am sick of working there."

"So quit."

"Are you sure?"

"Read my lips. Q-U-I-T."

"Oh, Meg. I think you're right."

"So does he." Meg pointed to a woeful Labrador pup who seemed to be listening to their conversation. So far they'd visited all the puppies in the store, as well as the kittens, the hamsters, even a few parakeets, and a boa constrictor. Meg didn't mind staying in there so long because it was the one place where she didn't think she'd run into Nick. And Celia had insisted upon staying because it was next to Greenberg's photo store, and she thought she might find Allie and L.P. Right at that moment, after her encounter that afternoon with Christopher and Whitney, Celia felt she needed all the support she could get.

"I'd still like to talk to Allie about it." Celia looked out past the kittens in the front window. Growing up, she and Allie had been inseparable, but since L.P. had come into Allie's life, Celia and Meg had become closer.

"It's okay, Cici," Meg advised. "I'll go with you. Just tell your boss that you don't want to work anymore."

"I guess I should. I've saved enough money to buy clothes for now, and could take an extra elective next semester — maybe business or marketing or something. I'd really like that," Celia concluded. But she didn't tell Meg exactly how much it had stung to be put down by Whitney. It was so humiliating having to fend her off from behind the counter of the Chili Place. Celia knew that it shouldn't have been, that it was just a job — but still, it made her feel stepped on, not good enough. And she swore that as far as Whitney Hain was concerned, she was never going to feel that way again.

Meg led the way to the door and peered into the mall. When she realized that she was just looking for Nick again, she turned back. "What are you afraid of? Your boss can't tell you 'no.' He can't make you keep working if you don't want to."

Celia's face relaxed as she realized that Meg

was right. This was her first real job, so she wasn't sure how it worked. "He can't, can he?" She brightened. "I don't know why I'm so nervous about it. It's up to me if I want to quit, right?"

"Absolutely." Meg held out her arm. "Shall we?"

Celia let her head fall back, and let out a happy howl that started the dogs yapping. Giggling, both girls hurried out of the store. They took off arm in arm with great purpose down the crowded mall.

"No more getting ice for Whitney Pain."

"Nope."

"No more burning my hands trying to pull bread out of that toaster machine."

"No more."

"No more cutting onions and grating cheese and stirring that chili till I want to puke!!!"

"Never again!!!"

They were practically running, and Celia was breathless and giddy by the time they made it back to the Chili Place.

Meg waited while Celia went behind the counter and found Pat, her round, bearded boss. Pat frowned and rubbed his beard as Celia nervously gestured and looked very serious. But after a few minutes, Pat shrugged and shook Celia's hand, and she came running back to Meg.

"What did he say?"

"He said he's very sorry to lose me, but he understands that sophomore year I need to give more time to my school work. I'll just work until New Year's."

"Perfect."

"Oh, and guess what! He said I could come back whenever I wanted and that he'd give me a recommendation!"

That struck both of them as hysterically funny, and doubling over, they giggled their way back down the mall, making up Celia's chili recommendation. She's hot stuff. She's full of beans. She can really dish it out. They laughed as they went down the escalator and past the big Christmas tree. By the time they reached the Unicorn Gift Shop they were reeling like two drunks. They went in because they spotted a statue of a Norwegian fisherman in the window that Celia insisted looked just like her ex-boss, Pat. Arms round one another, they entered the store laughing hysterically. Tears dampened Meg's cheeks and Celia's face was bright red. Meg skipped down an aisle stocked with stuffed animals, swinging her arms with her long legs flying. She saw the wooden back scratcher on the floor just before she stepped on it, but not in time to prevent her leg from shooting out in front of her. She let out a tiny scream and started to fall, but someone caught her from behind.

Meg gasped.

The someone was too substantial to be Celia. Two arms held her securely around the waist, and Meg smelled aftershave. She immediately thought of Nick and jerked away until she looked at the hands again and was even more startled. One was the head of Donald Duck. The other was Yoda. Her giggles returned.

"You're having too much fun, little girl," cautioned Yoda in a low, scratchy voice. It was a puppet. Whoever had caught her had a puppet on each hand. "Don't you know gift stores are serious places?" Now Donald poked her in the ribs with his beak. "That's right," Donald's quacky lisp answered. "Straighten up and look sharp," he slurped.

Meg finally got out of his grip and whipped around to see who it was. As she did, she spotted Celia watching, amused, from the other end of the aisle. Meg pulled back, caught the Yoda puppet, and slipped it onto her own hand.

"Oh, no, you've caught me. I'm melting. I'm melting," Yoda complained.

"Wrong movie," Meg laughed, trying to figure out if she knew this boy or not.

But Donald Duck was still blocking the boy's face. Meg held up Yoda, and the two characters fought it out. Finally Yoda's mastery succeeded, Donald fell to the carpet in defeat, and a bright face ringed by a mop of curly brown hair grinned at her.

"Jason! Jason Sandy!"

"Meg! Meg McCall!" he answered in his best duck voice.

"You're crazy."

"That's me." Jason winked. He was about her height and of ordinary build, but he had as much energy as an entire soccer team. It showed in the way he was constantly moving and in the way his brown eyes took in everything around him, as if he were afraid he might miss something. He was not quite handsome, but he had cuddly brown curls, huge, curious eyes, and a smile that was as quick as everything else about him.

"Hi." Meg caught her breath. "What are you doing here?"

"Just hanging out."

"Do you know Celia Cavenaugh? She's a sophomore."

Jason bowed, sweeping the floor with his hand. Celia smiled and said hello. It was then that Meg noticed another boy standing shyly behind Jason. At first she just saw his long, slender back. But when he turned around, she recognized his refined features and straight dark hair.

Jason stepped back to his friend. "You know Tim, don't you?"

Meg nodded. "Hi," she said softly. Tim's face was so sensitive, his slim body so graceful and quiet that Meg got the feeling that if she spoke too loudly, he'd bolt. He whispered hello, then put his hands in his pockets and stared at his feet.

"These puppets are great." Jason beamed. He'd picked two more off the shelf — Oscar the Grouch and Santa Claus. Without warning, Oscar flew over and started nibbling under Meg's chin. She shrieked.

"I was a grouch until I met Meg McCall," Oscar was saying, nibbling deeper and deeper into the crook of her neck. Meg's squeals swelled, getting louder and more shrill until a gray-haired woman in a smock whipped around the corner and scowled at them. She pulled the puppets off Jason's hands.

"This is a business, not a playground," she barked.

All four of them stared at the floor. Meg and Jason were stifling laughter.

26

The woman cleared her throat. "I don't think it's funny."

Jason, Tim, and Celia had already started up the aisle. Meg stopped to pick up the Donald Duck puppet and the back scratcher and place them both neatly back on the shelf.

"I'm sorry," Meg told the woman on the way out. "We put everything back." The woman put her hands on her hips and snarled until all four of them were well out of her store.

"How'd you like to be married to her?" Jason sighed, once they were out of the store.

"What a crab," said Celia.

Tim nodded once in agreement and shoved his hands even deeper in his pockets.

"So what do we do now?" Jason popped up, rocking on his heels, and looking around for a new adventure. His smile was excited and bright, and Meg found herself smiling, too.

Celia tugged the hem of Meg's blazer. We'd better go find Allie and L.P.," she said pleasantly. She gave the boys an apologetic shrug.

"You're going to leave us, and we've only just met," Jason said with a hand over his heart. Tim smiled but looked a little embarrassed.

"You'll survive," Meg said as she and Celia started for the escalator. "See you at school."

The guys waved. As the girls rode up, Jason raced over and tried to run up the down side. He finally gave up, yanked a flower from the artificial bed below, and tossed it up to Meg just before she reached the top. She stuck the plastic flower in her hair and waved good-bye.

"Who was that?" Celia said, amazed, as they

jumped off the escalator and began looking for the cookie store. The crowds had thinned out a little. They passed a mom who sat wearily on one of the benches rocking a stroller while her toddler whined and cried.

"Which one?"

"Both of them. Mainly that Jason guy. He's wild."

"Tell me about it." Meg stopped walking for a second. She couldn't believe that Celia didn't know both Jason and Tim. They were two of the best-known juniors at Redwood High. But, then, Celia never even wanted to hear about the Redwood athletic events she had so purposefully avoided all year, so it made some sense that she didn't know the two boys.

Celia had stopped in front of The Limited window. She was half examining the clothes, half perusing her own reflection.

"Jason's the yell king," Meg explained. "He does the most outrageous stuff. Don't you remember the Lawn Chair Brigade in the homecoming parade?" Meg smiled as she thought back to Jason in Tom Cruise sunglasses, flowered bermuda shorts, and a torn T-shirt, leading fifty kids who folded and unfolded lawn chairs with military precision. The Lawn Chair Brigade was his idea and the hit of the parade.

Celia took out her ponytail and leaned her head to one side to brush her hair. She'd changed out of her uniform into a pale blue sweater and pants, but she hadn't bothered until now to redo her hair. "I didn't go. I worked that afternoon."

"Oh. Right. But I'm sure you've heard of Tim. Tim Holt?"

Celia suddenly lost interest in her hair and turned to face Meg. "Him? That's Tim Holt, the basketball star? I've heard kids talking about him. But he seemed so shy."

"I think he is shy. He seems really nice, too. He's a great player. He's only a junior, and he's already one of the best in the league. Because of Tim we might even win the championship this year."

Celia put her brush back in her purse and sat down next to Meg. "Tell me more about him."

"Which one?"

"Tim."

Meg wasn't sure why Celia was suddenly so interested. Celia was staring at her with great purpose, like Meg had all the answers to the PSAT test. "I don't know him that well. I once rode home with him after a pep rally. He lives in one of those huge old houses near Nick."

Celia's eyes were getting bigger. "He lives in one of those Victorians on the hill?" That was where Whitney and guys like Christopher lived.

"I'm pretty sure. Why?"

Suddenly Celia was on her feet and back at The Limited window. She was fluffing her hair and pinching her cheeks and smoothing on a layer of lip gloss. "Let's go."

Before Meg could even ask where they were going, Celia was almost back at the escalator. Meg caught up with her, but not before they were already on their way back down. "Where are we going? We're supposed to meet everybody upstairs at Mrs. Fields."

Celia smiled and began to trot down the moving staircase. "It wasn't definite to meet Allie and L.P. there. We'll see them later. Come on."

Puzzled, Meg hurried to keep up as Celia bolted off the escalator and rushed along the mall. She would stop and look in store windows and alcoves, down narrow corridors, and into restaurants. Just at the point that Meg was going to demand that Celia tell her what they were looking for, Celia gasped. "There they are." She stood on her tiptoes, yelled, and waved. "Jason!! Tim!! Hey, you guys!!!"

Jason and Tim were standing in front of Taco Time with some other kids whom Meg didn't recognize. Jason was the center of attention, telling some kind of story, and Tim listened quietly from a few feet away. As Celia came rushing over to them, they broke away from the group to join her.

"Hi, again," Celia panted. Her cheeks were flushed, which made her look even prettier than usual. She gave Tim a huge smile, which he returned briefly before staring off at the Taco Time menu.

"I knew you couldn't stand to be away from us for long," Jason teased, looking at Meg.

"That's right," Celia broke in. "Listen, my cousin, Nick Rhodes, is having a big New Year's party, and I wanted to make sure that you guys know about it."

The boys stood up a little straighter, clearly flattered to have Celia make such an effort to invite them. "Nick invited me already," Tim said. Meg realized it was almost the first time he'd spoken that afternoon. His voice was soft and steady. "We're on the team together." Celia was staring at him like there was no one else in the shopping mall. Two crimson triangles appeared under his cheekbones.

"You're going, aren't you?" she asked breathlessly.

Tim shrugged. He clearly hadn't thought much about it and probably wasn't going to bother showing up.

"You have to go," Celia urged. She stepped in and touched his wrist. He watched her. "Will you?"

Jason joined Tim and reached up to sling an energetic arm around his shoulders. "Sure. We'll both go. I love parties. But the question is. . . ." Jason paused and grinned at Meg. "Will you be there?"

Meg felt the depth of his smile reach all the way down to her toes. She wished Nick were there to see. Giggling, she grabbed Celia and started to pull her away. "I'll be there," she called behind her.

Laughing again, Meg and Celia took off, running together down the center of the Redwood Mall.

CHAPTER
4

"Let's roccccccccckkkkkkk!!!"

By New Year's Eve, the Rhodes residence was a mad house. Allie and L.P. were hanging streamers and running up and down the hall, taping up posters they'd painted of 1985 old men and 1986 babies. Nick was moving furniture and helping his mom hide antiques she thought might not survive wild dancing, Celia was out back singing and skimming leaves from the swimming pool, Meg stood at the kitchen counter surrounded by two tubs of onion dip and the makings for a baker's dozen of cookies. And the whole time, Sean was testing the stereo in the sun porch and yelling like a D.J. gone loony. It was going to be a wild night.

Allie popped her head around the corner of the kitchen. She was in a baggy black dress with a huge sparkly scarf around her head. Meg thought she looked like a punk flapper. "Here's the rest of the tape," Allie said, holding out the roll and dancing to some weird new wave tune Sean had just blasted through the speakers.

Meg had sour cream in one hand and a sheet of hot cookies in the other. "Al, could you just put it in the drawer?" She started humming, too, as she put down the cookie sheet and flipped the cookies onto a plate.

"Sure." Allie hopped across the kitchen, opened the drawer, and tossed the tape almost to the ceiling. On the way down it plopped into the drawer just before she closed it. Allie giggled, then pointed out the window at Celia. "Guess she's looking forward to this party."

Both girls stared at Celia, who looked sensational in a new pink sweater dress, and was doing kicks as she tapped the leaves out of the pool strainer. Celia finally noticed them staring and waved. Allie grabbed one of the first cookies.

"How is it?" Meg asked.

"Mmmmmm. Great." Allie devoured it and took another. "You know New Year's is a great holiday except for one thing."

Meg brushed a strand of dark hair out of her eyes and tried to see back inside the oven. "What's that?"

"School starts again after the next day. Ugggggghhhhh!!!!" She pummeled the counter as if she were tenderizing a steak. "I want vacation forever."

"Vacation forever!" Meg joined in as Allie said it again. They put their arms around one another and laughed. Only Meg knew Allie wasn't kidding. For Meg, sophomore year had gotten more and more interesting — creative writing instead of routine English; biology, where you worked with real things in a lab; learning enough French to actually understand parts of a foreign movie. But she knew that Allie felt differently. It seemed the further along they went in high school, the less Allie liked it. She was having trouble in some of her classes and told everybody that she couldn't find her niche as a sophomore.

As if Allie knew what Meg was thinking, her excitement faded and a brief, lost look passed over her face. But as soon as L.P. appeared in the doorway, Allie's round face glowed as brightly as the full moon again, and she ran over, hugging him around the waist, and burying her face against his chest.

L.P. grinned and kissed the top of Allie's head. He was ready for this party, dressed in a pair of baggy striped pants, and a tie with a mermaid painted on it. He was big on antique and hand-painted clothing. "I'm going to help Mr. Rhodes get some ice. Do you need anything, Meg?"

Meg looked around the kitchen. "I don't think so."

L.P. started to go, but Allie hugged harder so he couldn't move. "I'll come, too," she said, beaming up at him.

"You don't have to." Just at that moment the doorbell rang. Sean yelled for Nick to get it, and Nick yelled back that he couldn't move because he was standing under a two-ton sofa. Meg started to go until she heard Sean's footsteps galumphing down the hall. "Maybe you'd better stay here and help answer the door," L.P. told Allie.

A chorus of voices exploded at the other end of the hall as Sean opened the door, and Nick yelled, "Hi, everybody, come on in," at the top of his lungs. It sounded like there were ten people at the door, laughing, screaming Happy New Year, flying down the hall.

Allie snuggled even closer to L.P. "I'll come with you. I don't like being at parties by myself." She seemed to clutch him harder as the happy voices and footsteps got closer.

"Meg and Celia are here," L.P. reasoned.

Allie gave him a little-girl look and shrugged.

"Okay." He gave in, kissing her on the mouth. He headed down the hall and reached back for her hand. "Let's go!"

" 'Bye, Meg! We'll be right back."

Before Meg could answer, Allie and L.P. were replaced by a score of Redwood bodies, ready to party. As they rambled in, Sean turned the stereo up so high, the whole house seemed to shake. The Swain twins started dancing in the doorway, somebody dropped ice down Meg's back, somebody else yelled that Jason Sandy was coming, so this party was sure to be hot, Celia came racing in the back door, and within ten seconds, two entire sheets of cookies had disappeared.

And so the night began. The doorbell rang so often, Nick ended up having to sit in a chair next to it. Finally, at about ten-thirty he took a break to enjoy the party himself. As he made his way down the hall he realized with a lift and a charge that his party was a huge success. The music was still so loud that the walls vibrated, there were so many kids dancing on the sun porch that the hanging plants jiggled, and the kitchen was so crowded that Nick hadn't even been able to get in and see if Meg was still there or if any of her food was left. Kids were yelling over the music, talking about vacation, the Grizzly basketball team, what they were taking next semester, and when Jason Sandy was going to lead his famous party games.

"Hey, Nick!" Sam Pond yelled, waving across the crowd. He was wearing a red-and-gold paper hat and tooting on a noisemaker. "Great party!"

"What?"

"GREAT PARTY!"

"Thanks."

"Have you seen Sandy?"

"I can't hear you."

"HAVE YOU SEEN JAS. . . . Oh, forget it." Sam laughed as Kirstin McGraw grabbed him from behind and tried to steal his hat.

Nick screamed about a dozen more "Hellos" and got about as many "Great parties" back as he squeezed his way through the dancers to see how Sean was doing.

He just missed being stomped on by Elise Howard, a girl on the newspaper, who was doing something that looked like a wild watusi. With his usual quick reflexes he got out of her way and also managed to evade the grasp of Hilary Tate, who tried to grab him and make him dance with her. Finally he found Sean, who was sitting on the floor, protected by a wall of stereo equipment and stacks of records. There was confetti on the top of his red head, and he was sorting through a box of albums. Nick crouched down next to him, and Sean looked up, his face tense with concentration.

"Sean, how's it going?"

"Good," Sean yelled back, pausing to adjust a dial on the preamp. He snapped his fingers and bobbed. "Have you seen my Oingo Boingo album? I can't find it."

Nick shook his head and thumbed through another stack. As he did, he noticed Jason Sandy dancing over. Jason was waving his arms and shouting along with the music. Nick was surprised to see Meg stomping and waving along with him.

"Hey, Sean," Jason hollered. Sean looked up. "How about some normal music. Don't you have any Paul McCartney or Madonna?" In rhythm to the music, he picked up the album cover to the record that was playing and spun it. It was The Bronsky Beat, one of Sean's favorites. "What's this?" he teased, looking at the back. Playfully he bonked it on top of Sean's head and yelled back at Meg. "Can you believe it? Even his rock and roll is brainy." Sean looked away, a little embarrassed.

Meg grabbed Jason and pointed him toward the hall. "Come on, Jason," she yelled. "Everybody's waiting for you in the living room!" Jason made a face back at Nick and Sean, then let Meg lead him away.

Nick stood up, following Meg with his eyes until their path was closed up by the crowd. It was funny. There were so many different kids here. Seniors and freshmen, jocks and student body officers, debaters and drama kids, at least half the Redwood High band, two exchange students from Japan, and almost all of the boys' and the girls' cross-country teams. But the one person who seemed to stand out — also the one person Nick couldn't remember inviting — was Jason Sandy.

Of course, Nick knew Jason. Jason always made up these amazing cheers on the spur of the moment, rhyming players' names or the current score. There was no missing his stunts on the football field that fall — like when Jason had arranged one time to have a real bear appear on the field at halftime. Even though everybody found out later the bear wasn't a grizzly and had been declawed, it created quite a stir.

Nick had decided not to invite any of the cheerleading squad because Celia had asked him not to invite Whitney Hain, but he was still glad that Jason had shown up. Jason had the reputation of livening up any party, and Nick thought that was great. Squeezing his way through the dancers, Nick went to the living room to see just what these famous party games that Jason was leading were. When he got there, he saw a game starting that was somewhere between charades and Name That Tune. Katrina Boldt, a tenor sax player in the band, was going first, miming "Girls Just Wanna Have Fun," and doubling over with laughter.

Nick spotted Meg first thing. He went behind the couch and crouched down behind her.

"Hi," he said right in her ear, feeling her silky hair against his face.

She turned back to see who it was, then jerked

away slightly. She was in a red blouse and jeans. She looked terrific.

"Hi. How's it going?"

"Good, I think." He rested his elbows on the back of the sofa, his chin on his hands. Jason was joining Katrina with huge windmill motions, and Meg laughed. "Nothing's broken . . . yet. And the neighbors haven't called the police. I guess that qualifies as a success."

"Sounds good to me." Meg clapped her hands as Jason asked for another song title. It was a minute before she turned back, as if she'd forgotten that Nick was still there. "I think everybody's having a great time." She clapped for Jason again as Katrina sat down. Now Jason was coming toward Meg. He was staring at her, his big eyes full of mischief, and Meg curled back into the sofa, giggling, and trying to avoid getting pulled into the game. She put her hands over her face, but Jason grabbed her anyway and pulled her in front of everybody while she blushed and grinned at him.

Nick watched her. He was starting to think that this game wasn't very funny. Actually, the more he saw of it, the more he thought this game was kind of dumb. He tried to catch Meg's eye to let her know that it was a dumb game, but she never looked at him. She just kept laughing and playing and acting like everything Jason did was totally hysterical. Nick wasn't sure why, but he was begining to find the whole thing very annoying.

At the same time, back beyond the swimming

pool and the barbecue and the apple orchard that separated Nick's house from Allie's — and even further back than the old tree house that the five friends had played in as kids — Celia and Tim Holt were taking a stroll.

"I'm so glad you decided to come to the party." Celia flirted, walking ahead of him over the fallen leaves and the hard dirt. There was a full moon, and the ranch land behind Nick's house went on for acres. They could walk all night if they wanted to. And from what Celia had seen of Tim, that was about how long it would take. She wondered it he was even interested in her or if her whole plan was a waste of time. "You were so late, I thought maybe you'd decided not to come," Celia persisted. She stopped under a branch, then held it as Tim bowed his tall frame to follow her.

"I was out in Cotter Valley," he said softly. The wind rustled his hair, and Celia watched as Tim pushed back another branch. Cotter Valley was a small, older town about ten miles from Redwood Hills. "I guess I lost track of time," he said quietly.

Celia stopped. They were in a small clearing, far enough from the house that the music was muted. The moonlight made shadows on Tim's face, and a tiny gust of wind lifted the sides of his dark hair. Celia decided that he was handsome. . . . Unfortunately he was reserved and shy, too. He'd even dressed formally in a pressed shirt, dark slacks, and a striped tie.

"What were you doing in Cotter Valley?" she asked, trying to get him to talk, to feel more comfortable with her.

Tim stuck his hands in his pockets and pushed leaves into piles with his shoe. "I coach some kids there."

"On New Year's?"

He shrugged. "They don't mind."

Celia leaned back against a tree. She was a pro at dealing with boys, but Tim wasn't giving her much help. "Look at the moon," she said finally. The cold wind was starting to cut through her. She still wanted desperately to start some hint of a romance with Tim, and she knew she might not have another chance. But if she didn't make progress soon, she'd freeze.

Tim looked up. The moon was beautiful and she could tell he appreciated it, but he didn't say anything.

"This part of town is so pretty."

Tim nodded.

She laughed. "But why am I telling you? You live over here, don't you?"

"Yup."

This was hopeless. Celia decided what she had to do; she just wasn't sure she had the nerve or the skill to pull it off. Holding her breath, her stomach full of butterflies, she walked over to Tim and took his hands. When he lowered his face, his eyes full of shock, she stood on her tiptoes and kissed him as fast as she could. It was a short kiss, a little awkward and stiff, but she'd done it. That was the important thing. She pulled away. The shock in his eyes had turned soft, almost hazy. When she rose to her toes again, he put one hand behind her back and stooped down to meet her.

This time when she tried to back away, he

wouldn't let her. He held her shoulders and pulled her so close that it was almost hard to breathe. Then he let her go and seemed embarrassed that he'd kissed her back so passionately. His cheeks were flushed with color, and his eyes searched every corner of her beautiful face as if he couldn't quite believe this was happening.

Celia was grinning inside, even though she kept her mouth in a straight line. She didn't want him to think she was laughing at him.

"Happy New Year," she whispered.

"Happy New Year," he breathed back.

They stared at one another. The moonlight gave them both a lovely silver glow.

"I guess we should go back," he said. He still hadn't caught his breath.

"Okay."

He took her hand and held it the entire way as they walked silently back to the house.

Wait until you see this, Whitney Hain, Celia thought over and over. Wait until you see this.

CHAPTER
5

"Countdown! It's eleven-fifty-four and twelve seconds!"

"Turn on the TV, bozo. We have to watch that big apple fall down in Times Square. It's not New Year's if you don't see that."

"I want my MTV instead!"

"I need a hat and a noisemaker."

"Pass the confetti!"

"What time is it now?"

"Five minutes and four seconds to go."

"YOOOOOOOWWWWWW!"

Meg was standing in the crowded living room, waiting, waiting, waiting for that wonder called midnight. She'd been yawning for a while but was fighting her sleepiness, at least until twelve o'clock. At that point, as soon as it was officially 1986, she would head home. No cleaning up, no wrapping extra food for Nick, no walking around the party and making sure that every person had a ride home and was doing okay. She was in too good a mood, and she'd had too good a time to wreck it by being Miss Do-Gooder again, no matter what Nick expected.

She looked around for her friends. From the new wave music that was blaring, she knew Sean was still manning the stereo. Allie and L.P. had gone next door to Allie's house when things started getting really raucous. Celia was sitting happily in the front room with Tim Holt. And Nick? Meg wasn't sure where Nick was now. He'd been playing the host for the last hour or so, flirting with the girls, joking with the guys. She found herself wondering who he would kiss in the madness of midnight, and then wondered why she was wondering about it. Luckily, at that moment, Jason plowed through the crowd to distract her. He was coming straight for her, and just looking at his mop of curls and wild eyes made her laugh.

"We only have three minutes to live," he said in a crazy voice, sweeping her into his arms before she could protest.

"What!"

"At midnight, no junior will be allowed to walk the earth."

"Oh, well I'm okay, then," Meg giggled.

"No, you're not," Jason reprimanded. "Sophomores are so selfish." He started to run with her, bolting so forcefully down the hall that Meg's arms and legs were smacking against people. He whispered madly, "the only solution is for me to be outside, under the light of the full moon when it turns 1986." Now he was doing his

Dracula imitation as he carried her through the kitchen and out the back door.

As soon as he got outside he lifted her over his shoulder. He wasn't much taller than Meg, but he was amazingly strong. "Jason!!" She kicked and screamed, but he held her securely, heading for the swimming pool, and dipping her head over the deep end.

"Meg McCall wants to be the first person to swim with all her clothes on in 1986," Jason teased.

"Jason!!!! Don't you dare!!" He was dipping her so far that her hair skimmed the top of the water. Meg was laughing and yelling and running out of breath all at the same time.

"That water looks so good."

"Put me down!!!" She beat against his strong back with her fists.

He inched closer to the edge. "Here we go."

Meg grabbed the collar of his rugby shirt and held on tight. "If I go in, you're going in with me."

He started to spin around and Meg closed her eyes, positive that the next thing she was going to feel was cold water and sharp chlorine. She prepared herself for the shock and clung to Jason, determined to drag him in, too. Then she felt him lose his balance, and they both began to tumble, leg over leg, arm over middle onto something much harder than water, something springy fragrant, and only slightly damp. She opened her eyes to see that Jason had spun away from the pool and the concrete, and they were spilled on a soft section of thick, lush grass. It was cold and the dew was already soaking through the back of her blouse, but Jason had toppled down next to her and he was very warm.

She rolled onto her back, and Jason moved in close, leaning above her on one elbow. He made a move to wrestle her, but she blocked him and started laughing hard. "Oh, no, you don't."

He held up one hand as if to prove that he was no longer on the attack, then he gazed into her face. His brown eyes lost their usual bright alertness and instead looked a little sleepy. Meg started to giggle again.

"What's so funny?" Jason demanded, pretending to be insulted.

"You!" Meg laughed. "You just make me laugh." She let herself go, sighing and laughing. Jason made her feel like a little kid.

He sat up and grabbed her arm, playfully pulling it behind her back. "Nobody laughs at Jason Sandy," he said in a voice halfway between Marlon Brando and Humphrey Bogart.

Meg was about to ask him who he was trying to imitate, when the party inside exploded. Horns began tooting, people were screaming. Meg and Jason sat up together on the lawn.

"It's 1986," Meg said.

Jason was looking at her with those sleepy eyes again. "You know the first thing I want to do this year?"

"What?"

He paused. "Kiss you."

He put a hand to her chin and closed his eyes.

At first Meg still wanted to giggle. Then his soft mouth met hers and they fell back on the grass and she felt so warm and breathless that giggling was the last thing she wanted to do.

Inside, on the sun porch, Kirstin McGraw was kissing Nick's cheek, and Hilary Tate was grabbing him so tightly around the neck that he thought he might choke.

"Happy New Year!!!" Hilary yelled, right in Nick's ear.

He blinked, wondering if his left ear drum had just been totally blown out. "Happy New Year to you, too." He untangled himself, and gently pushing the girls away, started over to Sean. Sam Pond blew a horn right in his face, the rolled-up paper part zapping Nick in the eye; confetti fell on his head; and somebody shook up a Coke can that sent sugary froth up his nose. He stepped over Katrina Boldt and Raoul Ramos, who had just fallen to the floor in a passionate embrace, and finally joined Sean.

"I didn't know they knew each other," Nick said, referring to Katrina and Raoul.

Sean tipped his head up to look. "They probably don't."

They both smiled.

"Have you seen Meg lately?" Nick inquired, realizing that he'd missed her for the last half an hour or so.

"I don't think so," Sean said. "I thought I saw her a while ago with Jason." He dipped into a bowl of potato chips behind him but came up empty-handed. He stood up and looked across the room. Kids were still hugging and screaming, blowing horns, and tossing the last of the confetti. "Could you keep the music going while I go to the kitchen? I'm starving."

"Sure."

Nick slumped against the wall as Sean left. Was Meg still hanging around with Jason? No. She couldn't be. Meg and Jason just weren't complementary types. He was all energy and pizzazz and nuttiness, and Meg was steady as a rock. You could count on Meg for just about anything, where all you could really count on Jason for was a joke. He'd seen Jason do some pretty crazy things . . . even some dangerous and wild things. Meg would go for that about like she'd go for a run without her track shoes.

"Nick, hi! Are you hiding over here?"

It was Sally Ann Stormis, a pretty blonde girl in Nick's social studies class, who everybody at Redwood agreed looked most like the stereotype of the California girl. Her blonde hair was straight and to her shoulders, her complexion tan, even in the winter, her eyes blue, and her movements light as a breeze. She laughed a lot and was really warm and everybody liked her. "Nah, I'm not hiding," Nick said. "Just filling in for our master D.J."

Sally Ann knelt and flipped through one stack of Sean's records, then she stretched a long arm and tapped Nick. "Well, this is a great party."

"Thanks."

"The music is really terrific."

"Yeah. Sean did a great job."

48

Sally Ann gave Nick a that's-not-what-I-meant look. "So how come you're not dancing?"

Nick didn't have an answer. He hadn't realized until right then that he hadn't been dancing. And now that the madness of midnight was subsiding, it seemed like the whole party was cramming in there for their first 1986 boogie. The whole party except Meg. And Jason Sandy.

Sally Ann was still staring at him, leaning on Sean's records and smiling.

"I'm not dancing, am I?" He remembered noticing at the last Redwood dance that Sally Ann was a great dancer.

Sally Ann swayed a little to the music, lightly tapping her blue jeans with her palm. "Nope. You're not. And the host is supposed to set an example."

Nick was flattered. He folded his arms, a little embarrassed, and was about to ask her if she'd like to dance with him, when Sean made his way back carrying a half-empty Doritos bag and a cellophane-covered bowl. "Nick," he said with a funny sound in his voice. "I just saw Meg, and she's, uh, *definitely* outside in the backyard with Jason."

Nick frowned. *Definitely outside with Jason,* what was that supposed to mean? But Sean wasn't explaining, he was just tearing into the chips and dip like he hadn't eaten for days. Nick stood up and headed through the dancers, stopping briefly to yell back to Sally Ann, "Look, I've got to go out for a second and talk to Meg. When I get back, do you want to dance?"

"That would be great."

"You're on," Nick said, pointing his finger and then smiling at her.

Nick squeezed his way past the people who were beginning to spill out and dance in the hall. Okay, he told himself, just go out and say hi to Meg. Maybe she'd even like to dance. They'd done it before at parties. Usually it was pretty late and they were really loose, but they always had fun together, and Meg could move in her stockinged feet like no girl he knew.

Nick went on down the hall, past the kitchen, which was pretty empty by now. Just cookie sheets sticking out of a sink full of suds, two overflowing bags of trash, and a bunch of empty dip bowls starting to turn brown and crusty. He peered out the windows first, seeing just the glimmer on the swimming pool and the Happy New Year life preserver that Celia had thrown in. He considered switching on the rest of the outdoor lights before he went back there, but something told him that he wanted to scope things out first before he made his presence known. He wasn't sure what Sean meant, but he *definitely* wanted to find out. It was a little sneaky, sure, but what were best friends for if they couldn't snoop on each other.

He slowly opened the back door, hearing it creak just a little, the cool breeze hitting his face and making him shiver. He could hear his own footsteps as he went down the steps, but that was all the noise he made, and the party was so loud he would have been covered anyway.

At first he couldn't see anything. He could smell the chlorine from the pool, the scent of

50

some of his mother's flowers, and he could see the palm tree that had always been in the backyard swaying slightly in the wind, but there was no horsing around or making Meg laugh like Nick thought Jason would be doing. He was such a clown, that guy. Nick had to admit to himself now that he was a little bit relieved he hadn't come out here to find Sandy really showing off to Meg and impressing her. It was none of Nick's business, really, and he couldn't isolate why exactly he felt that way, but he did.

Nick finally heard the slightest rustle accompanied by a little sigh of wind, or maybe it wasn't the wind. He turned and looked carefully; he lowered his eyes, and saw a shape near the blue background of the pool. It was on the lawn, a hundred feet away, so it was hard to see, but it only took a split second for Nick to realize what was going on.

"Meg," Nick whispered.

But it wasn't Meg alone; it was Meg with Jason. And they were down on the lawn with their arms wrapped around each other, and they were kissing. It hadn't started just this minute, either.

Nick took a sharp breath. He felt his whole body go tense, felt something tighten up inside, and something else drop like an elevator shooting down a million stories. He turned his eyes away as quickly as he could, walked back into the house, and silently closed the door.

CHAPTER 6

School started again just as it did every January. Kids yelled and screamed in the halls, throwing their arms around one another like they'd been separated for decades. There was the usual post-Christmas fashion show and the two or three broken legs from skiing. And there was that oppressive Redwood Hills fog and the slightly gloomy knowledge that the worst part of winter was yet to come.

Allie, Celia, Meg, and Sean met on Thursday, during morning break between second and third periods. They'd met at that time almost every day since they were freshmen. The only thing that was different today was that Nick wasn't with them.

But nobody mentioned Nick as they huddled together against the side of Allie's locker while she sorted through the junk inside — hats, scarves, a program from the fall play, a plastic sack of art pens, a pair of ballet shoes.

"Allie, what are you saving all this for?" Sean wondered, "the sophomore class rummage sale?"

"Leave me alone, Sean."

Sean rolled his eyes, and the other two girls looked sympathetic; at the same time they passed him silent don't-get-on-her-about-her-locker looks. It was common knowledge that Allie was crabby about being back in school and had been disorganized since day one. In fact, Sean was beginning to believe that she was one of those rare genetic specimens who had actually been *born* disorganized.

"Why can't I find it?" Allie complained, her voice rising in exasperation. "I know I put that computer manual somewhere."

"You didn't leave it in the gym?" Celia wondered innocently.

Meg started giggling. "That's where Celia would have left it. Or in the boys' locker room," she teased, elbowing Celia and rolling her head back like it was the best joke she'd heard all morning. Celia gave her a shot back with her shoulder, and the girls fell against Sean, almost sending him into Allie's locker.

"I don't get it," Sean puzzled with fake wonder, "what's in the boys'. . . ."

"Tim Holt," both girls said in chorus, and then they began laughing again. Celia blushed only a little bit.

"That guy?" Sean bluffed. The girls giggled harder when they heard that, and Sean almost cracked a smile himself. "Yeah, he's okay —

53

a good basketball player and everything — but I wouldn't want to go looking in his team locker for Allie's notebook. Talk about a gross-out."

Meg laughed again and tousled Sean's hair. "Well, gross-out or not, Tim Holt has the power to get Celia to her first basketball game, her first any kind of game, all sophomore year."

Allie was so shocked to hear that that she shot up and smacked her head on the inside of her locker. "Owww!!" Meg and Sean patted her. "Really, Cici?" Allie marveled, ignoring her head. "You're really going to the game tomorrow night?"

Celia and Meg grinned at each other and nodded at the same time while Sean shook his head. "Amazing," he teased, "this sudden interest in the game of basketball." They both gave innocent grins, as if he didn't know that Celia was after Tim Holt or that Meg was getting the hots now for Jason what's-his-name.

"Let's all go together," Allie decided, going at her locker again. "Wait a minute. Hold it . . . hold it. . . ." She'd ducked in and was going at the back of her locker like she was digging a hole. Then, just as quickly, she deflated. "Oh, shoot," she said, "that's not it, either."

Meg sighed, "C'mon Allie, don't you remember where you put it?"

Allie shook her head. Her new perm had gone wild from the humidity, and she was wearing these incredibly long earrings that kept batting her in the nose when she bent over.

"I see it, Al." Sean reached past the pictures that were taped to her locker door — Baryshnikov, Donald Duck, Bill Cosby, Meryl Streep, Georgia O'Keeffe, Julian Lennon. He pulled out a manual that was under about three inches of paper.

Allie wrinkled her nose as if the manual had a bad smell. "Thanks." She stuck it in her book bag and slammed the door shut. "Uhg."

"Oh, Al," Meg told her. "It's not that bad."

"Yes, it is."

"But Sean will be there to help."

"I don't care. I hate my computer class."

But no one was really listening. Meg and Celia were heading in the opposite direction, and Sean was getting a drink. "See you guys later!" Meg yelled, dodging a bulky senior, who wore about ten spirit buttons, all with the Grizzly paw print. "We'll save you seats at the game tomorrow night. Okay?" She hesitated. "Have you seen Nick?"

Sean yelled back, "No, have you?" his voice echoed over the voices and banging metal.

Meg looked at the floor, and Celia shook her head, then they scooted off together. Allie stood waiting for Sean, but he didn't budge. He still had this where-is-Nick look on his face that amounted to pure puzzlement.

"Sean, let's go," Allie urged dully. "We'll be late."

"I thought you didn't want to go."

"I have to, don't I?"

They moved down the hall, then out the door, where they tromped together across the quad, forging through the fog, which made everything look slightly dingy and out of focus, then past the old farmhouse that their class had made into a haunted house for their freshman fundraiser. Now it was being turned into a student art gallery, and there was a poster in the window announcing an upcoming art show and asking for participants.

Sean and Allie trudged on, then ran when it started to drizzle. They were both out of breath as they slipped into their chairs just as the last bell rang. Sean took his seat and Allie pulled up a chair next to him. "What am I going to do for this dumb first assignment?" she whispered, taking off her bowler hat and setting it in her lap. Her round face looked sad, her big eyes watery and lost.

Sean felt guilty that Allie hated the class so much. He should have known after she'd had such a hard time in Computer One that she wouldn't like it. But she complained about all her classes lately, and Thorson's class was one of the most interesting a sophomore could take. Plus, Allie had had no idea what she'd wanted to take instead. Thinking that he could really help her, Sean'd talked her into staying in computer class so he'd have the pleasure of her goofy company. But she hadn't been acting goofy or fun all week, and Sean felt bad that he'd talked her into doing something she didn't want to do. It bugged him that she could be so bored by something he found so fascinating.

After Thorson called roll, Sean pitched forward at his desk and tapped Allie's hand. Allie squinted at him.

"What?"

"I just had an idea."

"You have them all the time."

"Yeah, but this one is a good one. Al, why don't we do a computer art piece? Maybe we could display it at the art show in the Haunted House."

Allie sighed and twisted in her seat. Finally she looked back at him and, just for the briefest moment, Sean thought there was a hint of interest in her big brown eyes.

"No, c'mon," Sean persisted, "We'll work on it together. You come up with the ideas, and I'll do the programming." This was a great idea. Allie loved anything artistic, and maybe he could get her hooked on the computer stuff along the way.

"You mean we could do anything we wanted?"

"Well, almost."

Finally Allie got that goofy look on her face, and Sean smiled.

"Could we do a picture of giant tomatoes attacking Redwood High?"

"Only if Redwood wins."

She began to giggle. "How about a football game during the Ice Age?"

"That's a possibility."

"I know! You riding your mountain bike on top of Thorson's head."

Sean laughed. Thorson was totally bald. "Whatever you say."

A little while later they were all working on their projects, and Sean thought Allie was totally into it. She sat on the edge of Sean's desk while he keyed in commands. Both of them were staring at the video screen. They had decided on a picture of the Redwood Shopping Mall in the year 2090, complete with weird creatures and futuristic shrubbery.

"The one that looks like a blender," Allie said, leaning over and pointing, "can you make his head bigger?"

"It's a her." Sean bumped Allie's arm with his elbow. "I'll try."

Sean went back to his manual until his concentration was interrupted by a high-pitched beep. It was halfway between a doorbell and a dog whistle and was part of the school's fancy intercom system. Mr. Thorson went over and picked up the wall phone near the door. He listened, rubbed his head, and hung up.

"I need somebody to run a piece of software over to the office again." Mr. Thorson sighed. The two-year-old computer system in the attendance office had never worked right. Mr. Thorson was in the process of redoing it himself.

Almost immediately Allie lost interest in her work and shot to her feet. "I'll go." She waved.

"But wait a minute, Allie, we're not done," Sean complained, but Mr. Thorson was already at their monitor, and nobody else was willing.

Allie grabbed the disk and almost ran out of the room. Sean looked up at Mr. Thorson, then back at the screen in front of him. HI, THERE, he keyed in. MY NAME'S SEAN PENDLETON. WHAT'S YOURS? WE HAVE TO STOP MEETING LIKE THIS.

He banged the erase key and watched the screen go blank. He was alone again.

* * *

Meanwhile, Allie raced. She ran fast enough that Mrs. Brauner leaned out of the chemistry lab and yelled for her to slow down. She yelled back that she didn't want to get wet going across the quad, but by the time she got to the office her hat was so damp anyway, it was practically molded to her head. When she took it off, black dye leaked onto her fingers. Allie didn't care. She slapped the computer disk on the office counter and bolted out. Less than a minute later, she was in the library, searching every row and table for L.P.

She found him sitting at a long table in the corner, a mess of books open in front of him. He was resting his forehead in one hand and chewing on a pencil, his semi-punk hair sticking up in that little tuft in the front. Allie slipped in next to him.

Hi, she wrote on his notebook.

L.P. took off the wire-rimmed glasses that he'd gotten recently for reading, rubbed his eyes, and looked up, surprised. He had on Allie's favorite T-shirt — one he'd painted himself of an apple tree that bore faces instead of fruit. The paint was bleeding a little from the dampness, and there was a smudge of green on his hand. "What are you doing here?" he whispered.

Allie grinned and shrugged. L.P. had study hall third period and usually spent it in the library. That was part of what made Thorson's class so unbearable, knowing that L.P. was free and she couldn't join him. She leaned in close. "Some computer thing had to go down to the office again." She leaned her cheek on his sleeve.

He gave her a quick kiss on the top of the head, then checked his watch. "Al," he whispered, "you'd better get back to class."

"I can stay at least ten minutes. I ran all the way over here. I can tell Thorson they made me wait in the office."

L.P. sat up, so she had to move her head. "Come on, Al." He was whispering intently, trying not to attract the attention of the librarian. "You cut his class three times last semester. He's bound to figure it out."

Last semester Allie had had Thorson this same period. Same with L.P. and study hall. That was actually the reason she gave in to Sean and took the class again. She had to take some class that period, and Thorson's room wasn't that far from the library. "So what?"

"Al, you can't keep doing this."

"Why not?"

"You just can't."

"L.P."

"Shhh."

L.P. turned away from her, slipped his glasses back on, and tried to read again. His sudden coldness cut into Allie like a piece of broken glass, and she wasn't sure how to react. She could feel the pressure of tears, and she tried to hold them back. Even L.P. said she cried too easily. She made him look at her and tried to get him to smile, but his face was rigid, hard. Allie didn't know how someone she loved could look at her like that. The tears were pushing through, and there was nothing Allie could do to stop them.

60

She grabbed her hat, and not looking right or left, stormed out of the library.

L.P. caught up with her in the hall. He pulled her down past the audio-visual room where they could talk.

"What," she demanded, not looking at him.

"Allie, don't be mad," he pleaded.

"I make this huge effort to get out of class, and you don't even want to see me."

L.P. grabbed her shoulders. "I want to see you. I always want to see you. I just don't want you to cut class. Allie, you can't keep doing this. Sophomore year is really important for figuring out what you want to do. If I had goofed off all last year, I'd never know I was so interested in photography."

"You knew you liked photography before that. It's not my fault if I don't know what I want to do yet."

"I'm not saying you have to know, Al. Just try different things this year and give them a chance. See what you like."

Allie wiggled away from him. She hated this discussion. It was like when other sophomores talked about what they wanted to be when they got older . . . just the idea of that threw her into a panic. It was easy for L.P.; he had a talent. But how did people like her ever figure out what they were supposed to do? "Sure. See what I like," she repeated, "I like art, but I can't draw. I like ballet, but I'm a klutz. I like music, but I can't keep a tune." The tears came. Allie could no longer hold them back.

L.P. put his arms around her. "Oh, Al, don't

61

cry. I didn't mean to get in a fight. I just worry about you, that's all."

She let her hands encircle his slim back. His embrace was taking some of the pain away. She buried her face against his soft T-shirt and thought only of his arms and the safeness and the warmth. She might never have let go if a teacher hadn't walked by and cleared his throat at them.

They separated and started walking back to the library. "I'll go back at the very end of the period. Thorson won't care," she whispered as they sat back down at L.P.'s table.

L.P. smiled sadly and took her hand. "Okay."

Sean was anxiously waiting for her. He knew that Allie would visit L.P. and he didn't mind that, but he was pretty annoyed that she didn't think enough of their project to even try and come back early. He pressed one key and then another, but he'd lost interest, too, and the shapes on the screen did little to inspire him.

"Allie isn't back yet?" boomed a deep voice from overhead.

Sean looked up. It was Thorson. The teacher's bald head shone under the fluorescent light. "No, Mr. Thorson."

Thorson sat down in Allie's chair. He stared at the screen and then back at Sean. "Sean, I've been meaning to talk to you about something."

"Me?"

"You." Thorson smiled. "I sometimes get the feeling this class is too slow for you, that you're a little bored in here."

Sean figured he'd been bored half the time

since the first grade. He was used to it. Freshman year he'd been all excited thinking of the possibilities with new classes and teachers. Then this year he'd realized it wasn't going to be much different from middle school. But he didn't want to say that to Thorson. "Sometimes."

Thorson leaned forward on the desk as if he didn't want anyone else to hear. "I talked to the principal about letting you in a more advanced class, but he said there's no room. He won't let us bump up any kids until we get more equipment."

Sean knew that even though they had a lot of computers at Redwood, the demand to use them was so high that there were strict regulations about everything concerning the computer classes. "That's okay."

"So I've been looking into other things," Thorson continued, "and I found out about this class at the college. It's sponsored by the Exploratorium in San Francisco, and it's for gifted sophomores. It's not just about computers; it's all kinds of stuff, some physics, electronics, astronomy." He chuckled. "Last year I think they built a stereo system. Anyway, I can recommend you if you're interested. It's three days a week after school at Redwood College.

Sean wasn't sure how to react. The Exploratorium was sort of a hands-on museum — a huge warehouse filled with a million wonderful experiments that you could try for yourself. It was Sean's favorite place in the world. The idea of doing anything connected to the Exploratorium made Sean's mouth water, but the word "gifted" held him back. Wasn't gifted just the same as brain, weirdo, nerd? "Thanks, Mr. Thorson. I'll think about it."

Thorson stood up. "Just let me know. I have the application forms on my desk. The class starts soon."

Sean stared at the screen in front of him and wondered what he should do. The period was almost over, and everybody else was already gathering their things, turning off the computers, making plans to meet at the basketball game, then making their exits as swiftly as possible. Not eager to stand out, Sean turned off his computer, too and began to stack his books. There was a lot on his mind. Allie, Nick, the Exploratorium, the Redwood Mall in the year 2090. He was still thinking about it all when Allie rushed back in and grabbed her stuff before the bell rang.

CHAPTER 7

"Number twelve, playing center:
GUS BALDWIN.
Number seven, playing guard:
NICHOLAS RHODES!
AND PLAYING FORWARD FOR THE
GRIZZLIES: NUMBER EIGHTEEN,
TIMOTHY HOLT!!!!!!!"

The Redwood gym went crazy. Screams. Applause. Foot stomping. Someone tooting a kazoo and someone else banging a drum. Everyone together chanting EIGHTEEN, EIGHTEEN over and over and over. All of it ricocheting off the walls and the wooden floor until it seemed like the roof would blow off.

Jason was down front leading the group like a rock star. He clapped his hands, and the crowd followed him. He jumped up, and everybody rose to their feet. He threw a fist into the air, and the crowd screamed louder. When it seemed like the excitement had hit its peak, he pointed to a paper hoop painted like a huge basketball the cheerleaders were holding up. WHOOOMP. Suddenly the players were pouring through the hoop and the crowd was eating it up.

"VAPORIZE VACAVILLE!!!" Jason yelled.

"VAPORIZE VACAVILLE!!!!!" the crowd screamed back.

Across the court, the Vacaville Varmints watched nervously. Vacaville was almost twenty miles from Redwood Hills, but this was such an important game that hundreds of Vacaville students had made the trip. Whoever won this game took first place. Vacaville wanted to win, but they knew Redwood was hungry. In two years they hadn't won a single championship. Redwood could taste it.

"How are you doing?" Meg whispered to Celia between screams and cheers. They were both on their feet; Meg clapping wildly while Celia stood quietly next to her. Behind them L.P. and Allie stomped in rhythm, and Sean whistled through his teeth.

"I'm okay. I think," Celia answered.

The whole thing was pretty confusing. When Tim had first come onto the court, he'd smiled at her, and then ran ahead. That had bolstered her confidence. All week he'd found her between periods or at her locker to say Hello, Are you coming to the game, How are classes? It was clear that he liked her . . . a lot. Still, it was hard being here. Too many memories. Memories that made her feel like something hard and sharp had dug its way inside her. The countless times Celia had caught Whitney and her pals, Ann and Rebecca — both of whom were on the squad again this year — giggling and whispering and pointing at Celia, not even bothering to try and hide the fact that they were putting Celia down. It was ugly and it still made her boiling angry, but she had to put those memories away now and try to concentrate on the good things that were to come with Tim.

A boom from the crowd brought Celia back to the game. The gym was filled with noise — the pounding of the ball, the squeak of rubber-soled shoes, the crowd, and the referee's whistle. Tim was working hard, too — his straight dark hair flying every which way, but his handsome face calm and in control as he concentrated on the game. In his shorts and jersey he looked like an overgrown kid, so tall and relaxed — not muscular like Nick or bulky like Gus — but streamlined, graceful, and smooth as silk. Beautiful.

Vacaville scored two baskets of their own before Tim got the ball and tossed it underhand to Gus, who bounced it to Nick, who slipped it back to Tim. Celia knew Tim would make the basket, and she shot to her feet as the ball was leaving his hands.

"That's it, Tim!!!!" she yelled. A second later, the ball slid through, and the crowd started cheering.

But as Celia yelled, two people turned up to stare at her. One was a very handsome blond boy, sitting off to the side near the cheerleaders. He wore a ski sweater and a pair of Vuarnets around his neck, and kept standing, after everyone else was seated, to stare at her. It was warm and stuffy in the gym, but at that moment a chill went through Celia.

"Christopher," Celia whispered to herself. Meg looked over. "That's the guy I told you about from the mall," Celia finished.

"He looks like he uses hair spray."

Celia was grateful for Meg's joke and looked back down. The other person staring at Celia sat on the bench below, just next to the players. She was peering up, her tiny mouth set like hard candy and her gray eyes hurling icy daggers. Her dark hair was as fluffy as new wool, and she proudly tossed it away from her face. With all the strength she could muster, Celia glared back. It was about time Whitney noticed her, Celia decided. She wasn't going to hide her whole sophomore year. It was time for things to change.

Another basket was scored, and then time-out was called. That was the cue for Jason and the yell squad. They were out tumbling and yelling and cueing the pep band, when Celia saw Jason's eyes suddenly lock on Meg. A huge grin flashed across his face, and he dropped to one knee and pointed straight at her. "Log roll, log roll," Jason yelled. Everyone started laughing. A "log roll" was a famous Grizzly cheerleading practice that drove the teachers absolutely nuts. It had been instigated by Jason earlier in the year. Jason would point to somebody in the stands, and then the crowd would pick that person up and pass him or her straight-limbed, like a log, feet first, down to the floor. It was kind of like transporting a rolled up carpet, and it made everyone go into fits of laughter.

"Oh, no," Meg gasped, squirming self-consciously, and then she began to giggle as a dozen different arms reached for her, and she suddenly found herself being lifted into the air. "Celia, help! Wait a second . . . I don't want to do this. I. . . ."

Now the entire crowd was yelling, "LOG ROLL, LOG ROLL," and Celia could only watch as Meg was passed gingerly from row to row. She was giggling, almost hysterically, and the whoops and hollers were tremendous. Even the players on the teams looked up and noticed. Nick, in particular, was watching every move.

Finally Meg was set down in front of the cheerleaders on the floor. Her hair had fallen into her face and her cheeks were fiery red, but there was a big grin on her face and Jason ran over and gave her a hug. "Is she a winner?" he yelled through his bull horn up at the crowd.

"YESSSSSSSS!"

"Is she a Grizzly?"

"YESSSSSSS!"

"Are we going to win?"

"YESSSSSSSSSSSSSSSSSSSSSSS!!!"

Flushed, Meg began climbing on her own power back up into the stands. "That sure looked cool," Sean commented as soon as she'd sat down."

"Wasn't it scary?" Allie wanted to know.

Meg shrugged and laughed and did a shaky wave back as Jason blew her a kiss and then went into another cartwheel across the floor.

An hour later, the game was sewn up. The Grizzlies had won. Tim scored fifteen points and almost as many rebounds. He played brilliantly, and when the game ended, the entire crowd gave him a standing ovation as he trotted off the court.

"You want to go back?" Celia asked Meg excitedly.

"I guess. I'm supposed to wait for Jason by the entrance to the locker room."

"Come on."

Meg nodded and motioned to Allie and L.P. and Sean, who also got up and followed them down. They streamed onto the floor with all the other people, but Celia had to stop when she heard a high, clear voice call her name. She looked over to see Rebecca Steinmetz jumping up and down with her pom-poms, trying to get her attention.

"Hi, Celia!" Rebecca cried, pushing her way over. "How are you? I never see you any more."

Celia bit her lip and stayed cool. Rebecca had been on the squad with Celia freshman year, and she wasn't a bad person, just a follower — like Celia used to be. "Hi. Great game."

"Wasn't it? Isn't that Tim Holt something else?" Rebecca was practically swooning.

Celia was trying to figure out how to drop the fact that something else Tim Holt was interested in was Celia Cavenaugh, when Rebecca started heading away as quickly and as frantically as she'd appeared. "It's great to see you, Celia!" she was calling. "We're all going to the Bubble Café to celebrate. Whitney and everybody. Maybe I'll see you there."

Celia swallowed hard and thought to herself, Maybe you will, Becky. Maybe you will. Then she searched for Sean and Meg, finally spotting them down the locker room corridor amid yelling and commotion and hoots of victory. She rushed over.

"Watch it, Celia. I don't think you'd better go in there," kidded Sean, who stood almost at the door. "Even with this team you can only go so far."

Celia laughed and waited patiently. Pretty soon Tim emerged from the doorway, and she ran up and threw her arms around him. She had to get up on her tiptoes he was so tall, and she could smell soap and shampoo. She was surprised how light-headed she was when she came down, dizzy like when she spun in circles when she was a little girl.

"You were fantastic," she told him. She felt like she knew him a little better now, having seen him play. There was a grace, a beauty in him that moved her.

Tim merely shrugged. He was wearing a red-and-white striped shirt and a red V-neck sweater that made his wet hair look almost black in comparison. His cheeks were still flushed from the game, and his eyes were a dark, dark blue. He seemed oddly sad for someone who had just played such a terrific game. "I'm glad you came," he said softly. "Those guys from Vacaville can play better than that. I think they got psyched-out."

She took his hand, remembering what it was she had to do. The Bubble Café was where Whitney and the others were, so the Bubble Café was where she was showing up with Tim. "Let's go out and celebrate, okay?"

Tim looked around at Meg and Allie and Sean. They could see he was feeling a little shy. He smiled at them, but instinctively Celia moved him off a ways so they could be alone. "Do you want to?"

"Yeah. I do. I was hoping you'd wait for me."

That was the first time he'd really said anything to let Celia know how he felt about her. Hearing it filled her with happiness. "Really? Well, let's go to the Bubble. Everybody's going there."

The idea of joining the others seemed to make him gloomy again. "I thought maybe we could go someplace alone, like the Palace or somewhere. Just to talk."

"The Palace?" The Palace was a quiet, stuffy restaurant near the hills. With any other guy Celia knew it might be an excuse to get her on a deserted road nearby to park, but not Tim. Celia was fairly sure that if Tim said he wanted to go to the Palace to talk, that's exactly what he meant. The only thing she could think was that he wanted to avoid the crowd at the Bubble Café. She also knew there was no way she was going to date Tim Holt and avoid crowds. Especially the one gathered at the cafe tonight. "We kind of all made plans for the Bubble Café," she said gently.

He still looked worried.

"It'll be fun. Come on."

She took his hand again and he seemed to shrug off whatever was bothering him. "Okay. Let's go."

"Are you sure?"

"Positive."

They smiled and went further into the corridor, where even more kids were waiting now. They all congratulated Tim and hovered around him. Just then Nick popped out of the door.

"Hey, Rhodes, great game!" Sean yelled.

Nick smiled until he saw Meg, then he stiffened. He walked slowly over, not quite looking at her. His hair was still so wet it was dripping on the collar of his polo shirt.

"You waiting for Jason?" There was a tinge of belligerence in his voice.

Meg nodded.

"I figured that."

"Congratulations, Nick. It was a great game."

Nick looked disgusted. "Yeah, sure."

Meg'd barely seen Nick all week, and she couldn't believe how weird he was acting all of a sudden. He was looking around at the bulletin board, the equipment, the other players, the fans, anywhere but at her face. She felt like waving her hand to get his attention. "Nick, you played great."

"I did not. I almost fouled out." Nick shoved his hands in his jeans pockets and stared at the ground.

So that was it, Meg decided. Nick was punishing himself for getting four fouls. He had a tendency to take this kind of thing way too seriously, and when he got like this there was no getting through to him. "We're all going to the Bubble Café downtown. Why don't you come, too?"

He ran an angry hand through his hair, flicking off the excess water. "No, thanks." He started to leave.

Meg caught up with him. "Nick."

He kept walking.

"NICK!"

He stopped and faced her. For a moment neither spoke. They just looked at one another.

"Are you okay, Nick? Are you just mad because you almost fouled out?"

Nick rolled his eyes. "You could say that."

"You didn't need to play so hard, Nick. You were winning the whole time."

"Yeah? And what about you?"

Meg was confused. "What about me?"

"Maybe you shouldn't play so hard, either. That jerk Sandy could've broken your neck doing that stupid log roll."

Meg wasn't sure whether to laugh or get mad. "Are you serious?"

"He broke some girl's ankle during football. But, hey, if you want to go out with him. Go ahead."

"Nick. What is your problem?"

"My problem? It seems to me that it's your problem. Or rather, he's your problem."

Meg was backing up and shaking her head. She was steaming. This was typical of the way Nick saw her. Like she was his dopey little sister or something! Be careful, you might get hurt, stay away from the boys. Oooh, the more she thought about it, the madder it made her. It was just more proof of how he thought of her as Miss Boring and Conservative, who couldn't even deal with a guy like Jason. She faced him. "If you want to come to the café with us, Jason's driving. If you don't, I don't care."

Nick turned and walked away. "I'm sure you don't," he muttered to himself. "I'm sure you don't." Then he whirled around and walked out of the gym.

"Where's Nick going?" Sean asked, coming up to Meg.

"I don't know and I don't care," she spat out. "When's Jason getting out of there?"

Sean stepped back. "I don't know."

"Well, I wish he'd hurry." Meg put her hands on her hips and marched back over to join the crowd by the door.

"Touchy, touchy," Sean muttered to himself, wondering what exactly was going on. He saw Celia and Tim leaving by the side door, and Allie and L.P. waiting farther off to give him a ride.

"L.P.!" he yelled. "I'll meet you guys out in the parking lot in fifteen minutes, so don't leave without me. Hopefully Nick will be there, too."

They all nodded, and Sean went on his way.

Nick sat in his car, stared at the dark outside his windshield, and pounded the steering wheel with his fist. What was going on? He was acting like such a jerk. All week he'd been like this, playing so hard at practice, he'd go home with sore knees and bruised ribs. He'd picked on some poor freshman at lunch, blown up at his mom, and treated nice Sally Ann Stormis, who obviously had a crush on him, like she was an annoying bother.

He wasn't usually like this. He was used to being even-tempered and in control. His father had brought him up to deal with any situation coolly, and so far, he'd been able to do that. In track last spring he stopped a fight when two guys collided during a meet. He'd lost games, had guys give him an extra kick while he was down on the field, smashed into a parked car when he was learning to drive, argued with his father . . . but he'd never felt anything like this.

This feeling was dark and ugly and somehow connected to New Year's and Jason and Meg. Nick had considered the possibility that it was jealousy, but what was there to be jealous of? Meg wasn't his girl friend. She was the pal he had raced countless miles up and down Capitola Mountain. She was the dorky girl he'd bored with knock-knock jokes until she hit him with a croquet mallet. She was the one he'd built the tree house with when he was little. . . . How could he be jealous over a girl like that?

Nick heard a tapping on the passenger window

that made his heart speed up. He knew instantly it was Meg. He closed his eyes and decided what he would say. I'm sorry. I'm a jerk. I'll just not talk to you, and not see you for a while until this weirdness blows over, and we can be friends the way we used to.

"Nick."

It wasn't Meg. It was Sean.

Nick leaned over and unlocked the door. Sean slid in. "Everybody's going over to the Bubble. Aren't you coming, too?"

"No."

Sean leaned in, his tall slim body bending like a reed in the wind. "Look, don't be a martyr just because you made some fouls."

"What makes you think that's why I don't want to go?"

"I don't know." Sean's eyes got wide and Nick saw that super-intelligent look come over his face. Nick turned away. "This doesn't have anything to do with Meg and Sandy, does it?"

"Why should I care about Meg and Sandy!" Nick came back, too quickly and too loudly.

"Sorry." Sean held up his hands. "I just think you're acting pretty weird. Take my word for it. The last time you acted this weird was when I stole your Tonka truck when we were five." Nick didn't smile. "I'm here to talk about it, I mean if you want to talk about it."

Nick refused to look at him.

"Okay," Sean said, getting out of the car and slamming the door. "Suit yourself."

CHAPTER 8

"It's Jason Sandy and Meg McCall taking the last turn in the Indy 500."

"Jason!"

"In his vintage MG, constructed in an underground workshop by twelve midgets from Vacaville, he moves into second place."

"You're crazy!"

"They all said he was crazy, but he knew he could do it. Against insurmountable odds, he passes the souped-up Corvette and takes the lead!"

"JASON, SLOW DOWN!!!!"

Jason's convertible sportscar was flying up the curves of Capitola Mountain Drive. Meg clutched her seat belt so tightly that there was a red line indented in her palm. The wind made her eyes water. Hair flew in her mouth. Her body was jolted from side to side, and she was freezing. Still, she was trying her best to stay calm.

"Jason, this isn't even the way to the Bubble Café!"

The sportscar screeched to a halt halfway up the hillside. Jason turned to her, made a face like a mad scientist, and said in a gravelly voice, "I'm taking you away to my secret laboratory in the hills, where I am inventing the perfect woman. She will have your hair — " Jason touched her long hair — "your eyes — " he tapped her cheek — "your mind — " Jason scooted closer and kissed her forehead — "and a figure like Madonna."

Meg laughed and gave him a mock slug. "You are a total maniac."

"You must have heard that about me before, so don't say you weren't warned."

Before Meg could reply, she was thrown back against the seat as the car shot up the hill again. Jason hunched over the steering wheel and made the car swerve from side to side. It was a two-lane highway with a sheer drop over one edge. Meg was glad it was too dark to see anything besides the shadowy gray road, the thick forest on the uphill bank, and the expanse of glittery lights below. Just when she was about to demand that Jason stop fooling around, he zipped into a turnaround on the side of the road and shut off the motor.

Jason leaned back with his arms behind his head. The streetlight glimmered off his curly hair and drew a curvy line along the side of his cheek. "Look at that." He sighed, pointing to the view in front of them. Redwood Hills sparkled below like a Christmas tree.

Meg wasn't sure what to say. Part of her was still lurching from the ride. She was breathless and scared, and even a little angry. Another part of her was overwhelmed by the beauty of the view and by being up there alone with Jason. "Everybody's waiting for us at the café," she said. "They're going to wonder what happened."

"They'll figure it out." Jason winked. He slid down in his seat and slipped his arm around her.

His arm warmed her, and she liked the way his hand smoothed over her shoulder; still, she was glad the gearshift separated them. There was something about Jason that always made her feel slightly out of breath, one step behind. She wanted to be able to think for a minute and catch on.

"Do you always drive like that?"

"Only for special people." Jason winked.

"Jason, I'm serious. What's the speed limit up here?"

Jason grinned and shrugged. "It doesn't matter as long as there's nobody to catch you." He made his mad scientist face again and reached for her middle to tickle her.

She caught his hand. "Come on, Jason." He was so much fun, and he made her laugh like no one she'd ever known, but sometimes he went overboard. Like speeding up the Drive tonight, or earlier, when he'd picked her up for the log roll at the game. On the outside she'd giggled, but inside all she could picture was one wrong step and her head smacking into the benches.

Jason had relaxed and was now smiling at her with playful affection. He leaned toward her and rested his face against her cheek. "Don't be so uptight, Meg," he whispered. "I'm a good driver."

Meg sighed. Maybe she was just being uptight — being Meg the responsible one, the goodygoody, down-to-earth Meg McCall. That was just the person she was trying to get away from.

"I know," she whispered. "It's just dangerous. That's why they have rules about speeding." The minute she heard her own words she decided she sounded like one of her teachers. Ugh.

"What are rules, if not to be broken." Jason sat back and held up his hands. More seriously, he said, "Don't worry. I just believe in having a good time. Sometimes you have to break rules to do that." He nuzzled her shoulder. "You have to admit, I'm not dull."

"I never said you were."

He leaned forward and kissed her once. His kiss was the opposite of everything else about him. It was slow, delicate, and very soft. As he pulled away, Meg had to take a deep breath to keep the sky from spinning.

He turned the ignition key. "So you want to give all this up" — he gestured to the view — "for some crowded hamburger joint downtown?"

"Yes."

"You sure?"

"My friends are waiting for me. I have to see how Celia and Tim are getting along."

"I think he's nuts about her."

"Did he say something to you?"

"Tim almost never says anything to anybody. But I can tell."

"Well, I want to go see them. Allie and Sean are there, too." And maybe Nick, she found herself wishing. "Let's go."

"Madam." Jason grinned. "Your wish is my command." The tires screeched as he pulled back out into the street and sped down the hill.

The Bubble Café sparkled like an ornament that someone had forgotten to take down. Its windows blazed with light in a downtown that was otherwise dark and sleepy. There was music coming from the open doorway, and the smell of burgers and thick french fries, and the sound of a mixer whirling away on a vanilla malt. The waitresses, all in fifties pink, balanced huge platters, and hurried as quickly as possible up and down between the tables and booths. Meanwhile, what seemed like a thousand excited voices celebrated, and at the two largest tables, the Redwood High Grizzlies celebrated the loudest.

"Did you see the way this boy blocked that last shot?" Jason hollered in what was about the loudest voice in the entire cafe — and not caring one bit. He and Meg were standing behind Tim and Celia. Allie and L.P. were at the table, too, next to Sean, Sam Pond, Maria Martinez, the Swain twins, and about eight other friends and players.

"Yeah," Sean yelled. "That was so cool. It was like pure physics — action reaction, you know."

Everybody laughed, and Celia leaned her head into Tim's soft shoulder. She was surrounded by laughter and warmth and felt as light and happy as a helium balloon. At first all Celia had thought about was Whitney and her crowd, who sat at the other large table near the front. But in the midst of Jason's enthusiasm, Meg, Sean, and Allie's company, and most of all, Tim meeting her eyes and brushing her hand with his — it was almost enough to make Whitney and Christopher disappear.

"Vacaville didn't have a chance," Celia marveled, gazing up at Tim.

He gave a modest shrug. Celia wished that Tim was more excited. He was smiling, and looked pleased in his quiet way, but he wasn't nearly as charged up as Jason. But then who was? Jason could probably power the Hoover Dam if someone would hook him up during a Grizzly basketball game.

"Boy, that was a great game," Sean continued, just pausing to grab the communal plate of french fries that was keeping them all alive until the rest of the food arrived. From the way he was eating, you'd think Sean had just played a basketball game himself. "And that shot you took from about twenty-five feet out, how'd you know you'd make that?"

Tim looked a little embarrassed. "I don't know. I didn't think about it."

"Yeah," Jason repeated admiringly, giving Meg a playful nudge, "and I bet those guys from Vacaville can't *stop* thinking about it."

There was another huge laugh, and even Meg had to join in. As soon as they'd entered the cafe she'd forgotten about being upset over speeding or rule-breaking or anything like that. All she knew was that Jason was like nobody else in school . . . in the entire world for that matter. His excitement and enthusiasm were so infectious that Meg couldn't help but wonder if he'd have the café rocking and rolling even if the team had lost. He almost made her forget that Nick hadn't joined them. Almost.

"Well," L.P. said, in his usual thoughtful voice. "I guess this means we've finally got a shot at a championship."

"And it's about time," piped in Mcg.

"What do you mean?" Allie quizzed, pushing her curly bangs out of her eyes and licking ketch-up from her fingers. She thought it was great that they had won the game and that everybody was so excited, but for the life of her she could never figure out what was going on when they were playing. Usually she just cheered along with L.P. and Meg and hoped that they were right. It was the same with the standings in the league. She never knew who was in what place, or why it mattered so much.

"Come on, Allie," Jason prodded, "going to a loser school . . . who wants that? The point is to win. Get to the top, and stay there any way you can."

That cheer was greeted with raucous applause until the waitress came by with more food, and a dozen arms were grabbing and pawing through the shakes and the Cokes and the plastic burger baskets. Celia didn't even try to find hers — she didn't have to. Tim was taking care of it, and everybody was giving his long arms due respect. As he set the basket down in front of her, he paused for a second and everything stopped. It was the strangest feeling. Everything stopping like that. Just his dark blue eyes and hers and a pounding like surf inside, and everyone else disappearing. Then it ended, when a voice from the other table of Grizzlies finally overpowered theirs.

"OH, WHITNEY, THAT'S SO AWESOME!" the voice squealed at peak volume, and it was followed by a cheer as loud as any at the game. Celia looked over. Whitney and her crowd came back into focus. Their table was surrounded by so many pom-poms it looked like the floor was growing red and blue fur. Christopher was there and Rebecca and Ann, Gus Baldwin and Peter Temple from the team, plus about ten others — some of the richest and best-dressed sophomores and juniors at Redwood. Celia wondered if Whitney realized yet that she and Tim were together.

Celia's entire table got quiet as the *ooooh*s and *ahhh*s and *oh, Whitney*s continued to explode up front. Not wanting to flatter Whitney with her attention, Celia fixed up her hamburger and began to eat.

But then she was there. Whitney, deigning to visit their lowly table, all creamy-complexioned, perfectly fluffed, and daintily scented. She gave Celia a What-are-*you*-doing-with-Tim-Holt glare. At last. Celia pretended that she was ignoring her and kept on eating.

"Hi, everybody."

"Hey, Whitney," Jason said, putting his arm around Whitney and lifting her slim frame off the floor. Whitney glared at Jason and he glared right back. "Looking for a lap to sit on?"

Whitney rolled her eyes and shook down her gold bracelets as the guys at the table — excepting Sean — laughed. She wriggled away from Jason and gave him a phony smile.

"Excuse me," Whitney said, her smoky voice prim and polite. "I just wanted to come over and say congratulations to Tim."

Celia glanced up. And you wanted to see what was going on between Tim and me, she thought.

"Awwww," Jason swelled. "Isn't that sweet. Give the girl a hand, everybody." He went on, getting halfway out of his chair and talking in a corny game show host's voice.

Whitney tried to ignore Jason. Anyone could tell she was trying seriously to compliment Tim. Well, she should, thought Celia, and she should compliment me on having the good taste to be seen going out with him.

"Anyway, Tim, you were fantastic."

"Aww, Whitney, that's what all the girls say," Jason barbed.

Whitney tensed and scooted a few steps closer to Tim. Everybody was staring at her. "Well, go on and eat, everybody. I don't want your food to get cold." It was obvious that Whitney wanted to say something private to Tim, so everybody started eating, but kept listening. Whitney knelt on the floor next to Tim, her back in Celia's face. She leaned forward and whispered, "I'm having a party next Saturday, and I wanted to know if you could come."

"A party!" Jason screamed. "All right, Whitney! I love parties!" Whitney stood up, and Celia could tell she wanted to kill Jason. But he just smiled. Celia grinned at Meg — who was stifling laughter — then at Allie and Sean, who were also on the same wavelength.

"Well," Tim stammered, his eyes going to his plate of fries. "Thanks, but I'm not a great one for parties. I appreciate your asking — "

"Please," Whitney begged. Celia couldn't believe how much Whitney wanted him there. Tim must have just hit the top of Whitney's status list. "It's not like a regular party." Whitney looked around. "That's why I was being so private about it." She laughed nervously. "It's the opening of my family's new winery. There's going to be politicians and even some actors from Hollywood — the ones that are doing our new commercials — and a band and tons of food and my dad said I could invite whoever I wanted. . . ."

"Whitney," Jason interrupted, "If your dad said you could invite anybody, then there's no reason to be so private." He acted like this was a great discovery that would solve all Whitney's problems. It was great. Meg proudly hooked her arm in his. "So maybe you should invite all of us," Jason continued with a sweeping gesture that included the whole table. "Then I bet Tim would go. Right?" He stared down at Tim, and Tim grinned broadly for the first time that evening.

"Right, Jason. That's a great idea. How about if we all come?"

"What?" Whitney stammered. Her flawless complexion had gone chalk white.

Tim faced her, his back straight, and his dark eyes unblinking. "All of us here at the table. I'll come if they all do."

You could see that Whitney was almost choking as she looked around at Celia, Meg, Allie, L.P., Jason, and Sean. Celia knew what Whitney was thinking. Was Tim worth it? Was having him at her party a fair trade for having to invite low-life Celia; or Allie, who Whitney had called a loser freshman year; or Sean, who Whitney had said was a reject. And what about Jason, who was one of the only kids at school nervy enough to stand up to her, or Maria Martinez, who was overweight, or L.P., who had a punk haircut and hung out with the arty kids.

"Well, Tim, I don't know." Whitney glanced at Celia. "I mean, I already invited Nick Rhodes."

Celia rolled her eyes. Nick was rich and great-looking and incredibly popular. He might as well have been in Whitney's crowd, except that he wasn't a snob or a jerk. Inviting Nick was easy.

"Invite me," Tim repeated firmly, "invite my friends."

"That's right," Jason echoed. The other kids were now smirking and giggling at the proposal, too. Whitney hesitated. She pouted, she twisted her bracelets, she huffed. She glanced back at the table where Christopher and the other soshes were sitting. She looked as if she were trying to figure out how this was going to affect her social standing at Redwood. But in the end she knew she was beaten. It was better to have Tim at her party with a bunch of bozos than not to have Tim at all.

"Okay," she said in a surprisingly gracious manner. "You're all invited."

"All right"

"Hey, Whitney!!!"

No sooner had she said it, than Whitney wheeled around on her heels and was marching back to her table. It made everybody giggle some more, and the talk was all the more excited and gossipy as soon as she was gone: Could it really be? Had Celia actually witnessed Whitney-the-pain-Hain invite them to one of her parties? A fancy, sosh, winery opening for that matter. Would they really go? Celia said it was too good . . . certainly too good to miss. Jason said he wouldn't miss it for anything. Right then Celia decided that if Tim was going, then she would be there at his side. She would make Whitney swallow them as a couple until the rich girl wanted to scream. And every one of her friends would show up, too.

The whole discussion ended with another big cheer. But oddly, in the midst of all the hoopla, Tim had once again grown very quiet.

CHAPTER
9

An hour later when the two of them were alone, Tim was still quiet. He drove his stepfather's car, a huge, fancy Olds that had fuzzy upholstery and smelled new. The seat belt kept Celia clear on the other side of the front seat, and they both had trouble finding a decent radio station.

But as Tim approached Quemada Drive, just before her neighborhood, Celia forgot about the bad music and the funny adult car. It was then that it hit her that Tim had never seen where she lived. Her good sense told her that he wouldn't care — look how he had stood up to Whitney at the café. But her irrational side took over — the part that felt that his seeing her house, with its patchy lawn and peeling paint, rusty lawn chairs and astroturf leading to the front door, was like his seeing her with unwashed hair and splotches of Clearasil.

"You can let me out here," Celia blurted.

They were just turning off Central. On one side of the street was a motel, on the other a complex of doctor's offices.

Tim looked at her, confused. "Why do you want to get out here?"

"My house is just behind there." She pointed to an alley by the motel. "It's easier for me to walk through."

"I'll drive around."

She had her hand on the door. "That's okay."

"Celia, it's late. I'll take you to your door."

"No, I. . . ." There was no way out. She slunk down in the seat. "Okay. Turn right on Quemada." She tried to sound cheerful; after all she'd been flying high all evening. She knew it would seem weird to Tim for her to suddenly be edgy and evasive.

She directed him down two more blocks. "That's it," she said quickly, pointing to the smallest house. The porch light was on and shone down on the patch of astroturf. As soon as Tim pulled over, she saw the door swing open, and she started to panic. Her mother! Oh, no, please, no. Why hadn't she thought to have Tim drop her at Meg's house next door or Sean's across the street? Even worse, her mother had spotted them and was heading for the car. Celia went for the car door, but Tim caught here arm and stopped her.

"Do you have to go in right away?" he asked tentatively. "Um, there's kind of something I wanted to talk about."

Celia barely heard him. All she saw was her flaky mother getting closer and closer, her bathrobe flapping, and her hair tied on top of her head like a clump of broccoli. "I have to go. . . ."

"Celia, it's important. I don't know who to talk about this with, but I have to tell somebody. . . ."

They both froze when Mrs. Cavenaugh reached the passenger window.

"Hi, kids! How was the game?" Mrs. Cavenaugh asked in an over-loud voice that made Celia cringe. Her blonde bangs were singed with red — a recent experiment at the beauty parlor — but at least she was getting ready for bed, so she didn't have any makeup on. Celia had told her mother over and over not to wear all that eye shadow and frosted lipstick, but it never did any good.

Tim got out of the car and shook Mrs. Cavenaugh's hand over the roof of the car. "We won. Hi, I'm Tim Holt."

"I figured you were. Congratulations." Mrs. Cavenaugh bent down to talk to Celia, who was still slumped in the front seat. "I'll leave you two alone. I'm in the middle of this great TV movie with Joan Collins. Nice to meet you, Tim. Cici, come in soon."

As Mrs. Cavenaugh padded back into the house, Celia wrapped her arms around herself. Her excitement was totally gone now, flattened like something run over in the street.

"She's nice," Tim volunteered.

"Yeah. Right." Celia felt like such a sham. She couldn't imagine what her house and her mother must look like to Tim.

92

"Really. She didn't make a big deal about you staying out or anything."

There was a long silence. Finally Tim shifted, facing her with his long arm draped over the steering wheel. "Celia, how come you're so upset all of sudden?" His voice was soft, but he was staring at her intently, like he could see into her soul. For the moment, his shyness was gone.

"I'm not upset."

"Come on."

"I'm fine."

"Celia."

She sat up, smiled her best flirtatious smile, and tossed her hair over her shoulder. "What makes you think I'm upset? I'm terrific."

He looked away. It was funny, but he seemed to be uncomfortable again, put off. "You don't have to always be so on, you know."

"What?" Even though his tone was mild, Celia was stung by his criticism.

"I just mean that everything can't always be great." He paused and slapped his hand lightly against the dash, then stared out his window. For a while he sat like that and it was so quiet they could hear each other breathe.

"What do you mean?" she asked.

That sad look was back on his face again. "I just mean that sometimes it can look like everything's terrific, and you can act like everything's terrific, but really, it's not."

Celia turned toward him, surprised by what he was saying. Did he know somehow about the fear, the doubt that she carried just beneath the surface? "What would you know about that?" she said softly. "Everything's always been so great for you."

He gave an ironic laugh. "Yeah. Good thing I can dribble a basketball, because otherwise. . . ."

"What?"

"Nothing."

"At least you don't have to hide anything," Celia heard herself admit. She wanted to hold it back, but the pressure was building, and there was something about Tim that took away some of her fear.

"Everybody hides something. . . ." He hesitated. "Don't you think?"

Celia thought about her mother and their awful rented house and being put down for her thrift-store clothes and working that horrible job at the mall so no one could make fun of her clothes again. She couldn't hold back any longer.

"I can't even hide very well," she blurted. "It's so obvious."

"What?"

Celia closed her eyes and took a deep breath. The truth was like something hard and painful in her chest. "My mother. Where I live." Saying the words made her start to cry.

Tim immediately moved closer and put his hand gently on her wrist. "What about your mother?"

"I don't know. I guess I didn't want you to see her. She's so humiliating. You should have seen her at that parents' meeting this fall. She kept telling dumb jokes, and she was wearing this Day-Glo outfit like a teenager and comparing stuff at school to the beauty shop where she works. All the other parents were laughing at her, and she didn't even know it. I wanted to die."

Tim intertwined her fingers with his and held on hard. "At least she cares enough about you to go to stuff like that. My mom doesn't even come to my basketball games."

"What?" Celia wiped away a tear. She knew her makeup was running and she was probably a mess, but somehow she didn't care. "She wasn't there tonight?"

"She went with my stepfather to see his kids in Marin. They're fighting this big custody battle. He wants them to come live with us." Tim let out a sad laugh. "Sometimes I feel closer to those kids I coach out in Cotter Valley than I do to my own parents."

For a moment they sat quietly.

Celia faced him. "Tell me about them, the kids in Cotter Valley, I mean."

Tim slid down in the seat and looked at her. He smiled. "They're just normal kids, fifth- and sixth-graders mostly. It's more than just teaching them to play ball. I can help them have more confidence, stuff like that. I just know how to talk to them, I guess. It's hard for me to talk to a lot of people, but with them I always seem to know what to say."

Celia gazed into his dark blue eyes and got that crashing wave feeling again, like in the café. But there was something else, too. It was deeper, fuller. This feeling was very different from flirting or playing one-upsmanship with guys at the mall. This feeling was a little scary, like treading in clear, still water but also like floating in the air. She tried to smile. There was one remaining tear on her cheek, and Tim softly scooped it up as if it were something very precious.

Tim took her hand and their foreheads came together as if they could share the insides of their brains by touching like that. They sat very still for a while, even though Celia's heart was beating so loudly she was sure Tim could hear it. It was strange. She wanted to kiss him, to wind her arms around his neck, to be close, and feel the warmth of his skin. But she was unable to make a move. This was nothing like Nick's party, where she had thrown herself at him without a thought. Now, just to move her hand seemed too overwhelming a gesture.

Tim moved first. He raised his head and looked at every corner of her face. Her eyes, her chin, her forehead, her cheeks, her mouth. When he leaned in to kiss her his eyes closed, but Celia kept hers open. His face was so serene, so beautiful, that she couldn't bear not to look at it. But when his mouth touched hers, she had to close her eyes, too, otherwise she might have melted away.

He kissed her three times. When they stopped, Celia noticed his chest was heaving like hers.

"It's late," he said when they finally moved apart. When their eyes met this time he smiled. Really smiled. So did Celia.

She looked toward the house. The living room lights were flickering off and on — her mother's code for "Come in."

Celia wondered how long her mom had been paging her.

"I guess I have to go in. I had a great time."

"Me, too."

She slowly opened the car door and got out. Her legs were shaky. She turned back after closing the door. "Tim?"

"Hmm?"

"Before. You said there was something you really wanted to talk about. Do you still? Want to talk about it, that is." She wasn't sure why she was asking this. It just felt so good to talk about things that really mattered. And she suddenly wanted to know everything she could about Timothy Holt.

Indecision passed over his face. But the lights in the living room flickered again and he said, "It'll wait. Your mom's getting nervous."

"Yeah. I'd better go." She crouched down to meet him at the window. Tim leaned over, and she kissed him one more time. "Good-night." She walked slowly up the walkway.

He watched her. "Good-night."

Celia stepped onto the astroturf and turned back as she reached for the door. He was still watching her.

CHAPTER 10

SWACK. . . .

Tim banged his hand hard against the metal door and listened to it echo down the empty locker room. He could hear the ball still dribbling inside the gym — Nick Rhodes and Gus Baldwin playing one-on-one, a few shouts, groans of disappointment, and the pinging of the ball against the hoop. It was Thursday afternoon, only four-thirty. Practice was light that day since there was a game tomorrow. Coach Boyd had finished with them forty minutes ago. He, Gus, and Nick had stayed on to play for fun, but after a while the slap of the ball against the backboard had started to feel like a piece of wood being batted into his brain.

He wearily pulled off his sweat shirt and, letting it trail on the cement floor behind him, walked by row after row of gray lockers until he found his own. His pulse jolted when he saw that someone had beaten him to it. A familiar, curly-headed, energetic boy in a striped rugby shirt was leaning against Tim's locker, one ear to the door, fiddling with the lock.

"Jason, what are you doing cracking my locker?"

Jason looked up, embarrassed, but with that charming grin that made anyone forgive him just about anything. Tim didn't know Jason all that well — they'd only become friends this year — but he envied Jason's confidence and ease with people. "Shoot, you caught me," Jason laughed, straightening up. "I thought you'd gone home and I was safe." He kicked the locker. "I wasn't getting anywhere with this combo anyway. I used to be great at this in junior high." He spun the lock once more. "These new lockers are tough."

As much as he enjoyed Jason, Tim was in no mood to discuss cracking lockers. Besides, the idea of breaking into somebody else's locker was, for Tim, unthinkable. "So what are you doing?"

Jason sheepishly pulled a wrapped bundle from behind his back. "Celia gave this to Meg, who gave it to me to give it to you. I was going to sneak it into your locker. You weren't supposed to get it till tomorrow before the game."

Tim slowly opened the paper and unwrapped a red and blue hand-knit muffler. There was a note: *For the winner. From C.C.* The paper fluttered to the floor, and Tim slowly lowered himself onto the wooden bench. He clenched the scarf and leaned forward, almost dizzy.

Jason was leaning against the back of lockers

behind him and laughing. "She must sure be crazy about you, you lucky dog. What a knockout she is." Jason playfully punched Tim's arm, but Tim didn't respond. His shoulders were slumped forward, and he felt like he was slipping farther and farther down a steep cliff.

"What is it?" Jason asked easily, unwrapping a stick of gum and folding it into his mouth. "Don't you like her? I thought you did."

Like her? *Like her?* He was crazy about her. Nuts. At first he'd only been mildly interested. She seemed too aggressive and almost phony, but who could ignore a girl who looked like Celia? Then after the last game, when they talked in the car, something happened, and he thought he really might even be in love with her — whatever that meant. All week he'd bolted out of class just hoping to see her in the hall, everything in his body changing speed as soon as he did. He'd called her every night. But still, the one thing he'd wanted to talk about with her, he hadn't had the guts to bring up. And now, looking at her note — *To the winner* — he knew that he had pretended for too long that nothing was wrong. Very soon it was all going to come crashing down around him.

A booming laugh and the thud of the locker room door broke into Tim's thoughts, and he sat up.

"Better luck next time," Gus was taunting in his deep, foggy voice. A senior, Gus was a good player, but he was known for his bad temper and bullying attitude. He was one of those guys Tim would never have gotten to know if it hadn't been for sports.

"I'm just saving myself for tomorrow night," Nick teased, snapping a towel at Gus.

"Who cares about you? All we need is me and Holt, and we can kill anybody."

"Oh, yeah? I'd love to see that. . . ."

The two boys stopped ribbing each other as they turned the corner and saw Jason and Tim. Nick's face was red and his T-shirt was plastered to his chest. When he recognized Jason he flinched, but only for a second. "Hey, Sandy." Nick opened his locker, which was just across from Tim's, and sat down to untie his hightops.

Suddenly Tim stood up. He decided it was time. He put Celia's note and her present on the bench behind him as if he didn't want to look at it. He'd avoided this problem all of his sophomore year, and this first half of his junior. How much longer could this go on? He announced in a firm voice, "I have to talk to you guys."

Jason took his hands out of his pockets. Nick stopped untying. Even Gus, whose locker was in the next aisle, came back over. They were so unused to that kind of tone from Tim that they were all attention.

Gus, towel around his neck, one foot on the bench, spoke first. "Yeah? What?"

Nick and Jason simply waited. Tim looked at them one by one, and saw them as clearly as he saw the basket before a free throw. "What would happen if I was off the team?"

Silence. Awful, scary silence.

From the reactions of Gus, Nick, and Jason, Tim could have told them that he was getting married or taking a trip to Mars or planning to blow up the school. Nick looked worried. Jason looked shocked. Gus looked mad.

"What are you talking about, man?" Gus demanded in a voice that was almost threatening.

"Cool out, Gus," Nick snapped. "Tim, what's going on?"

Tim took a moment to breathe and think, or maybe to stop thinking, and then the painful truth he had been holding so deep inside came pouring out. "I'm on probation because I flunked algebra last semester. Bevins called me in the beginning of this semester and told me if I even flunk one test this term I'm off the team." Mr. Bevins was the boys' vice principal. He was tough, and on a new campaign to make sure kids didn't let their classwork suffer because of extracurricular activities.

"Bevins is such a jerk," Gus growled, kicking a locker. Gus had had his own troubles, barely maintaining a C average his sophomore year.

"Does Coach Boyd know?" Nick asked.

"Of course. I'm okay in my other classes, history and English and stuff. I told Boyd not to worry, there wouldn't be a problem. They made me take advanced general math this time, and it's not supposed to be so hard." Tim hesitated and grabbed Nick's towel to wipe his face. He was sweating more heavily than during the last quarter of a game. "But I'm still lost in it. We have our first test next week, and I know I'm going to flunk it. I just know it."

Jason shook his head slowly. "And if you do it's bye-bye basketball."

"Yup."

"Great," Gus barked. "And bye-bye league title."

And bye-bye everything that people think is important about Tim Holt, thought Tim.

But while the three of them were staring into space, already giving in to despair and defeat, Nick was thinking, pounding his fist into his palm and mumbling, almost talking to himself. Finally he turned to Tim and started firing questions at him.

"Who's your math teacher?"

"Kitzen."

"How much time before the test?"

"A little over a week."

"Are you willing to take the time to try and pass that test?"

"Anything, Nick. Anything."

Nick pulled on his Levi's and whipped a sweat shirt over his head. "I have an idea." He checked his watch. "We still may be able to catch him if we hurry. Come on with me."

Tim followed but looked bewildered. Gus and Jason trailed right behind him. "But where are we going?"

Nick held up a hand. "You'll see. Don't worry. We're not going to let you fail that test."

The four boys stopped in the gym entrance and formed a circle as if they were making a pact.

"That's right," Jason asserted. "The only thing that matters is keeping you on the team." He looked into each face. "And we're going to do whatever we have to do to make sure that happens."

They all shook hands and followed Nick out.

Sean was in the computer center, as he usually was after school these days, staring into a brightly lit video screen. He ran a hand through his red hair, looked up at the classroom, and thought how huge and hollow the room looked without anybody else in it. Even Mr. Thorson wasn't there; he was over in the attendance office working on the new system and wouldn't be back until he came by to lock up. And Allie, who was supposed to be working with him on this computer art project, had left over an hour ago when she realized that L.P. was out of his photography club meeting.

IT'S JUST YOU AND ME, BABY, Sean typed onto the screen. I SURE LIKE THE COLOR OF YOUR DISK DRIVES. Just as quickly, he erased it.

Allie'd left with the excuse that Sean needed to be alone to think and concentrate. He tried to explain to her that what they were doing wasn't that hard. She could probably do it herself if she ever took the time to read the manual. But Allie never listened when he told her that. Her round eyes would glaze over, and she would say that *Sean* was the smart one, and then leave Sean the smart one alone so she could go off with L.P. It wasn't that Sean was jealous or anything — he only liked Allie as a friend; he just wondered sometimes if being smart didn't mean spending your entire sophomore year with a video screen and a box of silicon chips.

"No offense," Sean said out loud to the computer, "but you don't even laugh at my jokes."

He rubbed his eyes, raised himself up out of the chair, and stretched. Out the window he could see the art studios and the big redwood trees mixed with the new plants put in last year and the clump of classrooms across the way. The sunlight was disappearing pretty fast. It was time to print out and start heading home on his bike. At that moment the door flew open, and what sounded like a herd of stampeding cattle burst into the room.

Sean turned around, puzzled, as Nick, Jason, Tim, and Gus Baldwin plowed in. Sean was glad to see all of them except Gus.

"You're still here," Nick heaved as he collapsed on the desk next to Sean. The other three hovered. They were all short of breath, as if they'd raced each other over.

"Obviously." It was strange to go so quickly from solitude to this. Sean felt surrounded. The four guys were staring at him with such expectation that it made him nervous. He quickly pressed a few keys to store his work in the computer's memory, then looked up at Nick.

"What's up?" Sean asked. It was pretty obvious that they hadn't come over to ask him if he wanted to shoot baskets.

Nick leaned forward. "Tim needs a math tutor. Right away."

Sean looked over at Tim, surprised. He didn't know why it should seem strange that Tim was having a problem with math — maybe he thought guys like Tim never had problems with anything.

105

"I have a test next week in Kitzen's general math," Tim volunteered in a serious voice. "If I don't pass, I'm off the team. Can you help me?"

Sean sat up a little taller. Tim was a junior, a guy he respected, and he and the others were coming for help that Sean was more than qualified to offer. Sean was already in advanced algebra, and he was very good at explaining things. At last being smart seemed important, valuable. "I guess so. Why not? Sure."

"All right!" Jason jumped and cheered.

"Don't celebrate yet," Sean warned. "It's not that simple." He turned to Tim. "I need to know what you're having problems with."

"We're reviewing basic geometry, but I'm lost," Tim admitted, embarrassed. "Once you get beyond adding and subtracting, I just don't get it."

The guys looked very serious again. They all leaned in, hanging on Sean's every word — except burly Gus, who stood behind them looking suspicious with his arms folded over his letterman's jacket.

"What math did you take last year?"

Tim looked away. "I had Geisslinger for Geometry Two." His voice trembled a little. "I had a really hard time because I didn't follow algebra very well before that. It was last period, and I used to leave early for sports all the time. I think Geisslinger passed me last year because he knew I needed to pass to play ball. Then this year Mrs. Kitzen figured out I didn't know what I was doing, and she, uh, showed no mercy."

Sean could tell that it was not an easy admission for Tim, and he respected him for telling the truth. "Do you have your book with you?"

Tim reached into his book bag and handed his text to Sean. As Sean slowly fingered the pages, his brain was getting fired up. He knew what he had to do and was excited by the challenge. "Okay. We'll have to get a book from beginning general math, too. You probably never got the basics, so of course geometry is like Swahili. We can work every night if you want, go through all the plain math stuff till you get it, then go on to right triangles, arcs, parallelograms — the stuff on your test."

Tim was looking more and more relieved. "Sean, thanks."

Nick patted Sean's back. "Did I tell you guys this was the man to come to?"

Sean smiled, filling with pride.

"I can see it's all going to happen!!" Jason added, so excited that he was kicking his legs against the desk. "Sean, you're sure he'll have all that by next week? Don't forget, that's the important thing, the test next week."

"I can't promise you'll pass the test," Sean told Tim. "I just know this is the only way to do it. You have to really understand the basics, or it just gets more and more impossible."

Suddenly Gus's deep voice cut in. "And what if he doesn't get the basics in a week?"

Sean faced Gus proudly. "Then we keep working until he does."

Gus put a hand on Sean's desk. "I don't think you understand what we're saying, Pendleton," he threatened. "We're telling you to make him pass the test. We don't care if he understands or

107

knows the basics or eats right triangles for breakfast. He just has to pass the test." Gus moved closer. "Got it?"

Sean glared.

"Gus, he knows what he's doing," Tim tried to explain in a patient voice.

"That's right, Baldwin," Sean insisted. He was not going to let this guy intimidate him.

"I know what he's doing," Gus exploded. "Young Mr. Spock here is acting like Holt has to study the entire encyclopedia to pass one stupid test." He threw his hands open and knocked a chair to the floor. "I'm telling you guys this is a waste of time! This guy's a nerd, an egghead. He's not gonna be able to help us."

The adrenaline rushed to Sean's brain as he shot to his feet. A nerd, an egghead, young Mr. Spock . . . is that what these guys thought of him, that he had pointy ears and was from another planet? He honestly wanted to help Tim, so he had tried not to remember how Gus had bullied him freshman year. He'd tried to block out that memory of Gus and three other older guys taping his body to the flagpole like he was a useless piece of paper. But that stinging humiliation was much too painful to ever really forget.

"Shut up, Gus," Nick ordered. "Sean's right!"

"You shut up, Nick!" Sean barked back, surprised by the force of his own anger. He'd pledged to himself a long time ago that never, ever was he going to let Nick defend him. Sean Pendleton stood up for himself, and he wasn't going to let his best friend take the flack while some overgrown bully with beef between his ears made fun of him. "Okay, Baldwin, have it your way," Sean spat out. His hands were shaking, but he managed to stand tall and firm. Even though Gus outweighed him by at least sixty pounds, they were almost the same height. "You know best. You get Holt through math. Don't look at me." He started to collect his pens and books with a furious sense of purpose.

Jason sprang to his feet, his teddy bear face full of panic. "Sean, wait! You can't give up. It's the school, the team's at stake. The first championship team at Redwood. That's what matters."

Sean glanced at Tim, who was hunched over the desk and was staring in front of him with troubled eyes. He had a moment of indecision. Tim needed him. Tim was a good guy. But Sean had his limits. He'd heard all the insulting names — nerd, egghead, reject, brain, geek, now young Mr. Spock. He wasn't going to take it, now or ever again.

"Gus said it," Sean told them as he pulled his computer disks out of the disk drives. "I can't help you guys." He slid them into the paper envelopes and put his manual away. He couldn't meet Nick's or Tim's eyes. "Good luck finding somebody who can."

The guys stormed out. Sean stared at the computer feeling bitter and guilty, and somehow caught in the middle of something that had nothing to do with him. Once they were gone, Sean nervously paced the room until he heard snatches of conversation in the hallway just outside the window. Sean crouched down by the heater and listened.

"What am I going to do?" Tim was asking in a voice that pierced Sean's heart.

"Don't worry. We'll think of something. Maybe I can tutor you," encouraged Nick in his hopeful way. Sean knew that would be useless. Nick was a good student, but hopeless at explaining things to other people.

"We have to do something," Jason was pleading like they were an unresponsive crowd at a losing game. "If Pendleton doesn't care enough about his school to help, then forget him. We'll have to figure out something else."

"That wimp," Gus grumbled, "that pathetic wimp."

"Shut up, Gus. If you'd kept your mouth shut. . . ."

"Hey, Rhodes, why don't you keep your mouth shut. . . ."

They were walking away and Sean was glad. He couldn't listen to anymore. He fought back tears, banged the table next to his computer, then turned his machine on again, reloaded, and began bringing his and Allie's art project back to life.

So far there were two creatures against a background of futuristic buildings. Sean moved one of them over, making it bounce its body into the other like an attacker in a video game.

"Take that, Baldwin," he swore, sending the other figure racing around the screen in terror. Sean followed it, keying in commands with his

110

fingers, all the time imagining running down and pummeling Gus Baldwin and every other big, stupid, overbearing guy that had made fun of him since he was old enough to show them up at anything that demanded using your head. Sean made the figures change shape, not caring that he was ruining his program. He added new commands, making the images violent and angry. Finally he banged both hands on the keyboard and heard plastic grinding against metal. There was a sudden flash across the screen, and then it all went blank. Erased. Zapped. Beat up. Gone.

Sean slowly took the disk out. He'd tell Allie tomorrow that he'd dropped the project, and that she was on her own.

But just before he left he thought of one more thing he wanted to do. He ripped a sheet of paper from his notebook and scribbled a note to Mr. Thorson. That program for gifted sophomores at the college? Sean cringed. Now he was a gifted sophomore. Junior year he could be head of the Science Club. By the time he was senior he could play chess all through lunch period, live after school in physics lab, and be the smartest kid in the whole stupid school. And the loneliest. Sean had to put a stop to it before it was too late.

He didn't give Mr. Thorson much of an excuse or an explanation. He simply wrote that he was too busy.

"Too busy," Sean muttered. "Too busy being a nerd."

CHAPTER 11

The next day Meg sat in the middle of the cafeteria going over the sophomore class's finances for about the twentieth time. They were trying to raise money to make a satin *Class of '88* banner for the main trophy case, but so far they'd only sponsored a Thanksgiving Dance that almost no one had attended. Meg was trying to figure just what they'd have left in their treasury after paying for the decorations and the refreshments and the band, but every time she tried to add up the numbers she forgot where she was and it all blurred in front of her. She chewed on her braid, crossed her new hightopped Reeboks, and groaned.

"Where's L.P. and his calculator watch?"

She pushed on the table to raise herself up and looked around. The cafeteria was just starting to fill. It was amazing how in a little over a year it looked so lived in. There was a huge mural of the mountains on one wall — painted last spring by the graduating seniors; the floor was scuffed and splotchy; one bank of lights in the ceiling didn't work; and there was a counter next to the regular caf line that in eighteen months had been named five different things — The Soup Stop, The Pizza Line, The Ice Creamery. It'd been voted vegetarian at the last election, and most of the kids called it The Rabbit Patch. Meg remembered that L.P. was sort of a vegetarian and watched the counter for him.

She didn't see L.P. and his calculator watch, but she did spot a blond boy in a letterman's jacket.

"NICK!!!" she stood up and screamed without thinking.

Then, just as quickly she sat back down. The boy turned around. It wasn't Nick — it didn't even really look like him, and her heart was pounding like a jackhammer. She knew the blood had rushed to her face, and she rested her cheek on her books. Why did she still think about Nick all the time? Was she crazy? Since school had started again, they were barely friends. And since the last basketball game, he stared right through her in class as if she were part of the blackboard. When she saw him in the hall, he glared and walked away as if she had done something horrible. Meg told herself that it didn't matter; she didn't care. Over and over she told herself that. Ha-ha. Look how much good it did.

Meg raised her head only when she felt two gentle hands on her shoulders. When she looked up, she saw Celia on one side and Allie on the other, both smiling. Allie's perm, slightly frizzy today, was sticking out under a gray baseball cap. Celia was in a pale yellow sweater and jeans, and she looked like a spring flower.

"Boo," nudged Allie.

"We found you," teased Celia.

Meg was really happy to see them. She was suddenly so glad it was them, and not Nick or even Jason or Sean. Sometimes boys were too confusing, and it was much better just to be with your girl friends.

"We bring an antinutritional blow-out from the student store," Celia sang, with a playful look in her blue green eyes.

Allie giggled and let down the front of her oversized black sweater. Tiny packages jumped out as if they were baby kangaroos. A Heath bar, red licorice, salted nuts, two boxes of Raisinets, a Snickers, and three Reese's peanut butter cups. Celia added one red apple. "Guaranteed to taste good, gross you out, and then make you pass out just when you need it. . . ."

Celia joined her, ". . . *in the middle of Lawrence's boring history class!!!*"

They all dug in. Allie first, pouring a whole box of Raisinets in one hand and gobbling them down. She adored junk food, and it showed in her slightly plump figure. Celia, on the other hand, was very careful about her weight and only picked at the bag of nuts. Meg ate absentmindedly. She jogged so much and played so many sports that she could eat just about anything.

"Thanks, I needed this." Meg sighed.

114

They all leaned toward the center, almost as if they were taking up the whole table so no one else could join them.

"Has Sean been here yet?" Allie asked.

Meg shook her head. "Why?"

Allie unwrapped the Heath bar and took an angry crunch. "You know that computer project we were doing?" Celia and Meg nodded and chewed. "Today in class he came over and told me he doesn't want to do it anymore. Just like that. No explanation. Nothing. Then after class, he left so fast it was obvious he wouldn't even talk about it. He can be so weird sometimes."

"All guys are weird," Meg muttered.

Celia started in on one of the apples. With the first bite it squirted on Allie. "Sorry." She handed Allie a napkin. "So what are you going to do for your computer assignment?"

"I don't know," Allie said grumpily. "It was only fun because of Sean. I don't feel like doing anything by myself."

They ate quietly, the giddy mood momentarily fizzled. All Allie could think about was facing that class without Sean's friendship and support. It was like sitting there when she knew L.P. was just a few doors away. It seemed as if this year her parents and teachers expected her to find some interest, some overwhelming passion, like L.P. had. But instead of feeling more stimulated by school this year, Allie just felt blah. Freshman year everything was exciting because it was new. She figured junior and senior years would at least have a sense of purpose because you knew college or a job was waiting at the end. But sophomore year was the eternal no man's land — no more novelty, no end in sight, just never-ending, never-changing blahness. And when you compared being with L.P. to blah, wonderful L.P. was going to win out every time.

"Guys *are* weird," Celia agreed. "Tim and I had a great time last weekend after the game." She looked off wistfully. "Really great. He called me almost every night this week. But this morning, when I asked if he wanted to do something after the game tonight, he said he had to go home and study."

Meg shrugged and borrowed Celia's apple for a bite. "Maybe he does."

"Sure." Celia took her apple back. "Who studies on a Friday night after a basketball game?"

"He's going to that party of Whitney's, isn't he?" Allie worried suddenly. "You know that's this Sunday afternoon."

"I wouldn't forget, believe me." Celia pushed the rest of her food away. "He promised he would. If he doesn't, I'll die."

"Cici, I wasn't going to tell you this," Allie looked unsure, "but maybe I'd better. This morning in gym I overheard Whitney telling some girls how Tim'll be tired of you really soon, how he probably won't even show up with you at her party."

Celia sat up, indignant. "She said that!!!"

"I didn't want to tell you, but I thought you should know."

"Ooooooo," Celia yelled, shaking her fists at the ceiling.

Meg and Allie glanced up, but there was so

much echoing laughter, clanging silverware, and music coming from the student store, that no one had noticed Celia's outburst.

"Meg, what about Jason? Is he still going?"

"I think so, Al."

"You don't sound very excited. I thought you liked him."

Meg couldn't respond for a moment. She did like Jason. Sometimes she thought she liked him a lot. He was just the kind of guy she needed, she told herself. Just the kind of guy to prevent her from being Meg McCall, do-gooder and student body heroine for the rest of her life. "I do."

"Guys are just weird," Celia repeated again, clearly lost in her own thoughts. "Allie, you're so lucky. You and L.P. have the only relationship that makes sense."

Yeah, Allie thought. It's the only thing in my life that does make sense. She sat there a little longer while Meg went back to her treasurer's report and Celia stared into space. She thought about opening her computer manual, or reading tomorrow's assignment for English, but it all seemed so futile. Grabbing the Snickers and the last Reese's cup, Allie said good-bye to her friends and went off to find L.P.

She knew exactly where to look. Down the main corridor, across the grassy quad, past the greenhouse and the rose bushes to the back art studio. Throwing open the second redwood door, she entered Miss Pittman's photo room. The walls were covered with black-and-white pictures — a bum in downtown San Francisco; Lisa Nyrop, an eleventh-grade beauty, looking wistfully out a window; a black-and-white study of a postage stamp, a thimble, and a leaf. That one was L.P.'s. He was experimenting with new subjects this year, finding ordinary things and then making them look weird or beautiful. He'd explained his theory to Allie, but she hadn't quite followed it.

Allie saw with relief that the red light over the darkroom door was off. That meant she could go in.

Dark. Even though L.P. hadn't starting enlarging or developing his pictures yet, he had the regular lights off and the special red light on. Allie didn't know how he could stand it, spending so much time in this tiny room with the chemicals that smelled like sour vinegar and that eerie red light. The room was so small, she was always afraid of crashing into something or knocking something over. Her worst fear of all was that she would open the door at the wrong time, let in the light, and ruin everyone's pictures. Allie had never done that, but she could imagine the fits that people would have if she ever did.

"Hi, Al." L.P. smiled, turning around. He was alone, wearing his glasses and a black vinyl apron that made Allie think of seals. It was so dark in the room, Allie thought, they might as well have been in a submarine at the bottom of the ocean. L.P. was fiddling with the enlarger, a contraption that looked to Allie like a huge microscope. Pulling down a yellow box of Kodak paper, he nodded to Allie.

"Could you get the 'Do Not Enter' light, Al?"

"Sure," Allie whispered, trying to match the

mood of the room. She squeezed her way back past the trays and the drying machine and the enlargers till she could reach the switch by the door. After she flicked it, L.P. removed a sheet of photo-sensitive paper and slid it into the enlarging machine.

She crept up next to him, her arm brushing his, and tried to see what he was doing. But he gave her a subtle nudge, as if she was getting in his way, but he didn't quite have the nerve to tell her. Allie usually avoided visiting L.P. in the darkroom for that main reason. It was the one place where he seemed not to want her around.

After exposing the paper to a few seconds of light, L.P. pulled it out of the enlarger and dipped it in the first tray of chemicals. With a pair of tongs he turned the paper and let the chemicals wash back and forth.

"What is it?" she asked, pointing to the photo paper.

He smiled, more relaxed now that the hardest part of his work was over. The actual developing was pretty routine, whereas the enlarging took real concentration. "Guess."

Allie waited. She had to admit it was exciting when he slipped a blank piece of paper into one of those pans of chemicals and the photo paper would begin to produce shape and texture and perspective until finally the picture emerged. That was like magic.

A circle filled with thin stripes was appearing, getting darker and darker as L.P. swished and sloshed.

"An earring?"

"Nope."

"A spider web magnified a hundred times."

"No."

"A piece of overcooked Spaghetti-O?"

L.P. laughed. This was a game they'd played in different forms since their first date. They were equally imaginative and loved to make up names and identities for anything they were unsure about. "Good guess." He pulled the paper out of the tray and held it up with the tongs and made a guess of his own. "A pizza cut into fifty slices."

Allie giggled, her old loud, goofy laugh, not holding back. That was the one thing she *did* like about the darkroom. It was one of the few places in Redwood High that actually felt private. "A Hula-hoop with bubble gum strung across it."

"No, a bicycle wheel!" L.P. announced, washing the chemicals off the photo.

"Really?"

Even the spikey tuft of L.P.'s hair looked proud. "I swear. It's the front wheel of Sean's mountain bike." He went back to the enlarger, almost knocked off the box of paper, then caught it with a sheepish grin. He held up his film to look for another shot. "I took it this morning in the parking lot." After finding the frame he wanted, he marked it with a fat red pencil. "He sure seemed bummed out this morning. Is your project going okay?"

Allie sorted through some pictures that were in the tray below the photo dryer — a doe-eyed child, a tree, a fashion shot — much less original than L.P.'s. "Not really. Sean decided he didn't want to do it anymore."

120

L.P. put his film down and stared at her. "Why?"

"I don't know." Allie kept sifting through L.P.'s classmates' photos. "He just said he messed up the program, so we're dropping it."

"Did you tell him you don't want to drop it?"

"He's the one who decided. It's not that big a deal."

The red light was shining across L.P.'s cheekbones, giving his narrow face a taut, angular look. "Al, you were interested in it. You can't just take stuff you're interested in and not finish it. You'll never get anything done that way."

Allie rolled her eyes. Not this again. She'd come to find L.P. so she didn't have to think about things like this. He was beginning to sound like her father. It was easy for L.P. He was consumed with photography, but she only felt that way about L.P. She walked over and tried to nuzzle her face against his shoulder. "Forget it. It's not important."

He flinched away. "It is important!"

His avoiding her touch made her feel icy and hollow inside. "L.P., I don't want to talk about this!" Her voice rang out in the tiny room. L.P. huffed with frustration and went back to his enlarger. "I'm sorry. I'll find something in school sometime. I just haven't found it yet."

L.P. huddled over the machine, stared into it, and shifted his sheet of paper. Allie knew he was annoyed at her, but she couldn't stand him ignoring her like this. She began to wonder if visiting him in the darkroom wasn't one of her all-time terrible ideas. "L.P., let's talk about something else, okay?"

He gave her the briefest glance. "Like what?"

She hated this! She couldn't stand fighting or angry words of any kind and felt the pull of tears even now. "I don't know." She leaned against the cold counter while he stared into the enlarger. By the way he kept cranking it up and down, moving the paper with sharp flicks of his wrist, she knew he was very upset, too. "Everybody's talking about Whitney's party." She tried to sound cheerful. "Celia made us all promise to go. It should be amazing."

L.P. stopped for a minute. "When is it?"

"This Sunday. All afternoon I guess."

He put a hand to his forehead and exhaled. "Al, this Sunday is when Pittman is taking a bunch of us to see that exhibit in San Francisco."

Allie was confused. She vaguely remembered L.P. telling her about some important photo exhibit he wanted to see. "You can go before."

"Pittman's driving. We're going at noon, and I'm sure we won't be back until night."

"Well, you don't have to go, do you? This party is really important. I promised Cici I'd be there!"

He had turned to look at her now, his face hard and set. "Then go. Celia doesn't care if I'm there, she just wants you. You go to the party and I'll go to the exhibit."

Allie was starting to feel woozy. The chemicals and the weird light and the close space were all getting to her. She knew L.P. just wanted her to be more independent, but the thought of going to that party with Whitney and all those other snobs without L.P. was terrifying. "I can't go without you," she heard herself say.

He said firmly, "Allie, I'm going to the museum."

The tears were starting to flow, and Allie was getting that scared I-don't-know-what-I'm-doing feeling she'd been getting so often lately. "Then I'll go to the museum, too, I guess," she babbled. "I'd like to go to see the exhibit. Celia can get along without — "

L.P. had grabbed her shoulders. He had taken his glasses off, and the anger in his eyes scared her even more. "No! I'm sick of feeling like we're tied together with a rope. We can't do everything together."

Allie stood there, for the moment glad of the red light because she knew every bit of blood had left her face. She felt like someone had just knocked her down until everything she had inside flowed out and she was left totally empty. They stared at one another, speechless, as the bell rang.

"Great," L.P. said shakily. He grabbed his paper out of the enlarger and slapped it in the first pan. "I'd better get this through so you can leave and go to class."

"I don't care if I'm late to class," Allie pleaded. She heard a few kids rambling into the photo room on the other side of the door. "I just can't believe you said that. You don't even like me anymore, do you?"

L.P. turned back to her. "Al, that's not it. I like you. I even still love you. I just can't be your

123

whole life. It's too much." He turned back to the pan.

"I think maybe you don't want to be a part of any of my life from the way it sounds."

"Allie."

"And I think that sounds just fine to me!"

She threw open the door just as L.P. was taking the papers out of the first bath of chemicals. The light flooded the tiny room and she saw L.P.'s face clearly, the rage burning in his eyes as he flung his ruined photo into the garbage.

Everyone in the classroom stared at her as she ran out of the darkroom, the red light flashing over the door like some kind of awful alarm.

"Allie!" Miss Pittman reprimanded. "Don't you know you're not supposed to open that door when the red light is on? You've just ruined someone's pictures."

Allie stopped in the doorway, the tears spilling down her round cheeks. "If you want to know the truth, Miss Pittman," she heaved, not looking at the teacher, "I really don't care."

CHAPTER 12

"Tim, do you get it?"

"I don't think so."

"You know, now that I think about it, it doesn't make much sense to me, either."

It was Sunday morning and Nick and Tim sat at Nick's kitchen table. They were both staring bleary-eyed into Tim's open math book. Outside it was cold and bright, and the sun flooded more and more of the old kitchen as the afternoon went on. But no matter how light it was — how much the pool glistened or the trees sparkled — inside Tim's head it was still a blank.

Nick rubbed his eyes and padded over to the fridge. His feet were bare and the floor was cold, but he was much too preoccupied to care. "I'm not helping very much, am I?"

Tim, looking weary in a gray sweat suit, his hair sticking up from the way he leaned his forehead in his hand, answered, "It's not your fault, Nick."

"I'm sorry."

"It's me. I just don't get it." Tim bent down to pet Hughie, Nick's dog, who was lounging under the table. When he raised his head again, a slant of sun cut his hopeless face in half.

Nick did okay in math and he was sure he'd be able to help Tim, but he just seemed to make it more and more confusing. Like figuring out the third side of an isosceles triangle — he knew how to do it — *if* he didn't think about it too much. But once he started explaining it, he couldn't believe he'd ever passed geometry himself. He leaned back against the refrigerator and drank milk from the carton. "Darn."

Tim closed the book with a whack, and Hughie barked.

"Calm down, Hugh," Nick ordered, snapping his fingers. "The person we need is Sean." If only Gus hadn't been so stupid and insulting. Nick couldn't blame Sean for refusing to help, he just wished Tim and the team didn't have to be the ones to pay for it.

"Thank your folks for me," Tim offered.

Nick shrugged. His father was so excited about the team that he'd actually stayed home from some political dinner to help Tim Friday night after the game. Nick's mom had given up her volunteer duties to help this morning. But it was a joke. Nick figured there must be something about this math stuff that made you forget it as soon as you graduated. Even his older brother Jack, who was home from college for the weekend, couldn't do geometry anymore. "How about your stepfather? Doesn't he do something with engineering?"

"He went to see his real kids this weekend." Tim waved a hand as if to say, It doesn't matter anymore; What's the point. Nick knew he'd given up. "Maybe you should go to that winery thing and forget about it."

Nick opened the fridge and stared into it. He wasn't hungry. He just didn't want Tim to see his face. The idea of Whitney's party did not cheer him. In fact, it made him feel worse. "You going?" he asked, not looking back.

"I guess. Celia really wants me to."

"Yeah." Nick figured that Meg would be there, too, and that was what bothered him about Whitney's dumb party. Meg would be there with Jason. Even this morning when he'd looked out the window at that patch of grass where he'd seen them kissing on New Year's Eve, he'd felt sick to his stomach. He'd convinced himself that it wasn't jealousy. He just cared about Meg, and there was something about Jason he didn't like. He couldn't pinpoint it, but something about Jason Sandy didn't seem worthy of a girl like Meg. At least that was what he told himself. He slammed the refrigerator door shut just as the front doorbell rang.

Tim looked up. Hughie trotted down the hall. Nick heard his mother open the door and welcome whoever it was in her super-polite voice. The next thing he knew, Jason Sandy and Gus Baldwin were standing in the kitchen doorway.

"Hi." Jason grinned, rubbing his hands together and looking much too happy, especially compared to Tim and Nick. Gus stood behind him in the doorway, looking around uncomfortably at the antiques, as if he was afraid he might knock something over. They were both dressed up: Jason in a pressed shirt with suspenders and a bow tie, Gus in cords and a V neck sweater. They were probably on their way to Whitney's party.

"Where can we go to talk?" Jason whispered excitedly, looking back down the hall.

Nick and Tim looked at one another. "We can talk here."

Jason shook his head. Whatever he had to say, he was about to burst with it. "Somewhere private. Very private."

Nick tried to figure out what could be so secret as he found his running shoes under a chair and pulled them on. He gestured out the back door, trying not to look at that place on the grass where Jason and Meg — "Outside. By that old tree house."

The boys filed out quietly, Hughie following, like they were on a CIA mission. Single file they circled the pool and ducked under one of the apple trees, until they stood at the base of the old oak that held the tree house Nick and Meg had built when they were kids. Gus dropped his heavy body over Hughie's doghouse. Nick realized he didn't really like having these guys out here near what was kind of a special place.

Jason looked around to make sure no one was nearby, then crouched down on the dirt and fallen leaves. Nick leaned back against the tree trunk and Tim stood with his arms crossed, his face still pale and hopeless.

"Okay," Jason began in an intense whisper. "I figured out how to solve our problem." Gus was nodding and smiling.

Tim looked up. "You mean me and Kitzen's class?"

Jason flashed his charming smile. "None other." He looked at Gus, then back at Tim. "Do you know Roger Sandler?"

"Sort of," Tim answered. "He's in my English class."

"He's in your math class, too." Jason grabbed a stick off the ground and pushed some leaves as if he was going to make a diagram. "Except he's not in your period. He has Kitzen first, and you have her fourth. Right?"

"Yeah."

"And Sandler is very interested in helping us."

Tim and Nick stared, not too sure of Jason's meaning.

"Yes?"

"Don't you get it? Sandler takes the test first period and before he hands it in, he makes another copy of the answers. Then we get those answers to you at morning break, and you memorize them or write them down on your arm or something, then you go in fourth period and pass the test."

Tim went white.

"It's perfect. Kitzen always gives the exact same test in both classes, and Sandler's a B student. See, you don't want somebody who gets all the answers right, because then Kitzen might suspect something."

Nick couldn't look Tim in the face. He could just picture Jason and Gus talking Roger Sandler into this. Roger was one of those bland, semi-popular guys who'd do anything to impress somebody he thought was cooler than he was.

Jason waited for a reaction. When none came, he stood up and held out his hands. "So what do you think? Is it a great idea or isn't it?" Tim was still staring in front of him in hopeless despair. Jason walked over, put his arm around Tim, and bolstered him. "Tim, it's just one test. Don't get freaked out. Kids do this all the time. Think of it as a way to buy time. Okay?"

Still, Tim stood motionless. When a broad leaf floated down and landed on his shoulder, he made no attempt to brush it away.

"Look," Jason continued, "the important thing is the team. Think of the game Friday night. Did you hear that crowd, man? You were a hero. Think about next Friday. We're against Napa. If we beat them, we sew up the title. We sew it up! But we can't do it if you flunk Kitzen's stupid test and get thrown off the team."

Gus was staring at Tim's face, trying to see if Jason was getting through. It was hard to tell. Tim's refined face was still pale and without expression.

"Think about it, man," Jason persuaded. He was facing Tim now, looking up into his face with enormous purpose. "You can either be a hero again next weekend, or you can be a failure."

130

Finally Tim reacted. He flinched and met Jason's eye.

"That's right, man. You can be Tim Holt basketball star, or Tim Holt stupid junior who can't even pass dummy math. Which will it be?"

Tim's body went taut, and for a moment Nick thought he was going to punch Jason. But instead, he turned away and muttered, "Okay. You're on."

Jason clapped his hands and hooted, then looked around to make sure nobody was near. "All right!! I knew you'd think it was a great idea." He patted Tim on the back. "Don't you worry about anything. I'll take care of it all. You just meet me during morning break on the day of the test." He held out a hand to shake, but Tim ignored it. "Great," Jason laughed, aware of the slight. "You'll thank me later for this." Jason backed up, smiling at Tim and Nick and gesturing to Gus. "We gotta go, you know, get to that party of Whitney Hain's. Come on, Gus. Meg's waiting for me. I told her I'd meet her there."

Gus jogged slowly over to join him. Jason waved and yelled back as they headed around the pool toward the back of the driveway. "I'll see you guys later at the party. Don't worry about a thing! Grizzlies forever!!!"

Finally they were gone. Tim and Nick stood very quietly. Even Hughie had retreated into his doghouse and gone to sleep. Just the rustle of the leaves, a few birds, and Hughie's soft snore.

"Are you going to do it?" Nick asked after what seemed a long time.

"You mean cheat?"

Nick looked up, surprised by the bluntness of Tim's answer. "You don't have to."

Tim responded in a dull, flat voice, "What other choice do I have?"

Nick wasn't sure what to say. All he knew was that his reasons for not liking Jason Sandy were stronger than ever.

CHAPTER 13

"Are you sure this is a shortcut?" Sean asked, shoving forward the brim of the bicycle cap he'd worn for the hike.

"I'm positive," Celia snapped, turning around and frowning at him. The two of them, along with Allie and Meg, were tramping across an open field on their way to Whitney's. They'd been walking for almost an hour, from near downtown to the north end where they picked up Allie, then off the main road, and along the back way to the Hain winery. They'd passed countless rows of grapes and cows and narrow streams, and a barn that was so old it didn't even have a roof anymore. But finally, as they reached the crest of a small hill, they heard the faint buzz of an electric guitar, the boom of a bass, and the thump of a set of drums. The party.

Celia stopped, jumpy now that they were getting close. "Hold it a second, you guys." The hem

133

of her lacy dress stuck out below her coat and she checked it for burrs, finding three. After picking them off, she examined her new flats and her stockings. No mud. By some miracle the ground was fairly dry, although she was dusted up to her shins with a thin layer of dirt. She bent down and brushed herself off.

Allie glumly picked a puff weed and blew it, hesitating first to make a wish. She was dressed in a short skirt, huge dark sweater, jockey's cap, and high heels that were obviously painful on the uneven ground. Meg was the only one who really looked comfortable in her usual hightops, jeans, and blazer.

"Why didn't we get somebody to give us a ride?" Allie complained.

"We're almost there," soothed Meg.

"That's right," Celia barked. "It's not that bad. Come on."

They resumed walking. Celia hadn't meant to take her anxiety out on Allie — who was in a bad enough way already — and she immediately felt guilty. Besides, she hated having to walk even more than Allie did. But for some reason, Tim had called that morning saying that she should go ahead without him; he had something very important to do and would meet her there later. Are you sure you'll be there? she'd asked him, trying not to sound desperate. Yes, yes, he'd assured her. She prayed he was telling her the truth.

Jason had called Meg with a weirdly similar story. What were all those guys doing this morning? Probably working out some dumb strategy for the game against Napa, or something else that guys got caught up in when they were as close to a championship as the Grizzlies were. Celia'd tried Nick, too, but her aunt said he was outside somewhere and would have to call her back, which he never did. So what was Celia supposed to do? Phone everyone she knew with a driver's license until it got back to Whitney that Tim hadn't even bothered to pick her up? Never. She could only pray for the day she got a license herself and walk over, pretending they did it on purpose for their health. She just hoped that Tim would show and make it obvious to Whitney that he was still crazy about her.

Celia hurried up next to Allie and touched her arm. "I didn't mean to yell at you, Al. I'm sorry."

Allie looked up at her, her eyes teary. "I know. I'm just such a wreck." She sniffed.

Celia felt awful. Boy, was she a jerk to be anything but super-nice to Allie. Allie had plenty to hurt about. "Did you talk to L.P. this morning?"

"I'm never talking to L.P. again."

Meg joined on Allie's other side. "You okay, Al?"

Allie nodded sadly.

Sean hurried up alongside her. "You sure?" When Allie made a point of ignoring him, he fell back, content to bring up the rear.

The three girls linked arms as the chalet-shaped Hain winery came into view.

"I'm so glad you guys came," Celia told them. "If Tim doesn't show up, I'll die. I can just hear Whitney telling everybody how he dropped me because I'm such a lowlife."

"Don't worry," Meg counseled. "He'll be here.

He's crazy about you. Jason said so." Meg stopped as they got closer. The music was loud now, and the wine-tasting room was straight ahead. It looked like a cross between a fancy barn and a ski lodge, and there were tons of people, some of them very dressed up. There were flowers and banners, and a camera crew from the local news team was filming out front. Whitney's father was being interviewed, and he had his arm around Whitney as if she were a prize-winning vintage. "Is Nick coming?" Meg asked, then wondered why she'd asked it.

"I don't know," Celia replied, arranging her hair and taking a deep breath before their final descent. "You guys ready?"

Meg and Allie nodded. Grasping hands, the three girls started down the hill. "You know," Celia said, looking back but not seeing Sean, "I'd never be able to do this if we weren't all together."

They marched down and Sean followed. He watched their backs, Meg's athletic gait, Allie's wobble, the one burr that was still stuck to the hem of Celia's coat. He heard every word they said, and he could certainly tell them more about what was going on than they could tell each other. But did they ever ask him? Not a chance. He was practically the invisible man, and since he'd given up on Allie's project, it was like he'd been thrown into the dumpster. It was almost as if Allie blamed him and that dumb project for her break-up with L.P.

Sean looked up at the clear, cold sky and wondered why he was even going to this party. He wished that L.P. or Nick or Tim or some other guy was there with him. It wasn't very often that the girls made him feel like a fifth wheel, and he considered stopping them and talking about it. But with all the weird stuff going on, maybe it was better to hang back and not say a word.

They went down, down, down the grassy knoll, running at the very end into the packed parking lot, then walking more slowly around the side to where guests were being escorted out of their cars by some man in lederhosen and knee socks. Between all the hiking and the guy in green shorts, it made Sean think of Boy Scouts, another thing he couldn't exactly share with the girls. Then Whitney Hain noticed them, swooped over, and Sean felt even more out of his element. Out of an instinct directly related to sheep, Sean huddled closer to the girls.

"Uh-oh, brace yourself," Celia said, "here comes Miss High-and-Mighty herself."

"I wonder if she ever thought we'd really come," whispered Meg.

Allie pulled her hat over her eyes. "I'm beginning to wish I hadn't."

The girls stood in a line with Sean slightly behind them.

"You came!!" Whitney sang, her husky voice so sweet it almost made Celia gag. Whitney had her hair piled on top of her head and was in some long velvet get-up that made her look like a maiden in distress.

Whitney held a long-stemmed glass containing something impossibly pink and frothy. She waved it like a scepter and coyly bobbed from side to side as if Celia were hiding something behind her back. "Where's Tim?"

Celia tried to keep her cool and think fast. "It's such a nice day, we decided to walk over. Tim's meeting me here. He had practice."

Whitney's gray eyes locked onto hers. "On Sunday?"

"Can't have too much practice when you have an important game coming up."

"And when you're the most important person on the whole team," added Allie, finally getting up enough nerve to speak.

Whitney smiled, a victorious, cocky, infuriating smile. "Well, the other people from Redwood are in the back room — we can't go in the main room with all the wine — so you should find some people you know back there" — she paused and giggled — "just in case Tim stands you up."

Celia's eyes glistened like two snowflakes. "Don't worry. Tim'll be here soon."

"He'd better be." Whitney paused to wave to Christopher, who stood in the doorway in a white *Miami Vice* sport coat and his Vuarnets. He also held a glass of that pink frothy stuff and toasted Celia with a slick smile. Celia's insides were starting to tumble and churn.

Whitney turned her attention to Meg. "What about Jason, my dear yell partner?" Her bow mouth bunched up. It was almost as bad as the way she'd sneered at Jason all through the game on Friday. Then she noticed Allie and turned on her real venom. "Gee, it looks like none of the girls in this crowd can get her guy to show up with her."

Meg noticed Allie's eyes start to water again and wanted to smack Whitney for zeroing in on her. But just as she was about to give their hostess back some of her own, she heard Jason's boisterous voice boom from the parking lot.

"MEG!!!"

He was running, practically leaping, accompanied by a much more subdued Gus Baldwin. Jason looked even more plugged-in than during the last minutes of a close game. His eyes shone and his curly hair was flying. As soon as he reached Meg, he lifted her off her feet and swung her so wildly, she accidentally kicked an elderly couple that was walking by.

"Whitney, my favorite cheerleader," Jason said smugly, noticing Whitney and putting Meg down. He bowed and kissed Whitney's hand, then looked her up and down, appreciating her princess outfit. "You waiting for Prince Charming?" He winked and held out his arms. "Here he is."

"Spare me, Sandy." Whitney picked up the train of her velvet dress and turned around. She walked up a few steps toward Christopher, and then turned back like Bette Davis in some ancient movie. "So glad you could all make it. Have a great time." After a grand exit, she and Christopher disappeared into the winery.

Meg fell into Jason's arms and started to laugh at the way he'd put Whitney in her place. Even Celia was smiling, and Allie's tears were gone. Sean had taken a few steps back, clear to the other side of the entrance from Gus, and they all looked at one another, not sure what to do next.

"Well, would you like to see my castle?" Jason asked in his best Dracula voice, gesturing toward the winery.

Meg laughed some more. She wasn't sure what it was about Jason that kept her always off balance, always surprised, always not quite sure what to expect. Whatever it was, and even though it sometimes made her uneasy, right now she was very glad of it. Taking his arm, she gave him an impetuous kiss on the cheek as they marched up the steps to look for the Redwood room in the winery and join the party. Allie, Celia, and Gus followed.

Only Sean stayed behind. Alone.

Half an hour later Jason was still flying. He was ticking like a time bomb, not able to stand in one place or think about anything but Tim and his brilliant plan to save the day for the Redwood Grizzlies. He wanted to tell Meg about it, but he got the feeling that she wouldn't approve. There was something about her — a straightness, a toughness, that could be a downer. He was still crazy for her long dark hair and those crystal blue eyes and terrific legs, but sometimes he felt like she didn't know how to . . . let go.

So he'd snuck outside while she was comforting Celia and Allie, both of whom did not look like they were having a good time. Now *he* knew how to have a good time. Anywhere, anytime, anyway, Jason Sandy knew how to take the roof off life and have fun.

Even here, he thought, looking around him at the trash cans and the edge of the parking lot and the stacks of empty wine crates. He was out behind the back door, the grungy back entrance to a small kitchen and the storage room. This was a place that was definitely not on the tour for the more distinguished guests.

Jason laughed as he pulled the two ruby-red bottles out of his jacket. He and Gus had lifted them from some crate in the hallway when none of the adults were looking. He didn't know anything about wine but figured if he drank fast, he could get tipsy, then be back with Meg before she even knew what happened.

"Psst. Sandy!"

Jason looked up, at first alarmed, then relieved that it was only Gus, who'd gone to filch a corkscrew. As Gus tiptoed out, he held up the silver tool and grinned.

"You can open it," Jason instructed. He was a little embarrassed to admit that he wasn't sure how.

Gus knelt down, peeled off the wrapping around the cork, and twisted the corkscrew in. He wrenched hard with his wrist. Half the cork came out in his hand. "Shoot. Crappy wine," he grumbled. Checking once to see if they were still alone, he jabbed the corkscrew in again and again until the half cork shot down into the bottle and red squirted up over the neck. Gus caught some of the liquid and licked his fingers. He grinned. "Want the first sip?"

"After you."

Gus chugged it, then gasped for air, and handed the bottle to Jason. "It's pretty sweet."

Jason took the bottle, and imitating Gus, drank

as much as he could. It went down surprisingly easily. It actually tasted good, better than he remembered the sips he'd had with his parents at restaurants. With a second swallow he decided it was much better than that grape-juice-ice-cream concoction they were serving the kids inside. The bottle was still at his lips when he sensed the presence of a third person in their midst. He slowly lowered the bottle, trying to decide what to tell the waiter or adult guest who had caught them. For once Jason was a little nervous and merely attempted a charming smile.

But it wasn't an adult or the hired help. It was Sean.

"What do you want, Pendleton?" Gus asked belligerently, standing up.

"Yeah," Jason prodded, "you going to go in and tell on us? You'd probably do something like that." He brazenly took another drink. "Guy who won't even try to help his team."

Sean narrowed his eyes. He'd been wandering around the party alone, just watching and thinking. The girls were huddled together — Allie in despair over L.P., Celia freaking because Tim still hadn't shown, Meg taking care of them and flirting with Jason, but every ten minutes asking if anybody'd seen Nick — and all of them ignoring Sean and acting like he couldn't possibly understand.

The smartest guy in the sophomore class, and he can't possibly understand.

"So what are you going to do, Pendleton?" Gus threatened, "Go tell your mommy on us for being bad boys?"

Sean stood tall and pulled his sweater down over his cold hands. Maybe if he were dumb, things would be easier. Maybe if he were insensitive and stupid like Gus. Or thoughtless and pushy like Jason. Maybe now that he was a sophomore he should learn to be just like the other guys.

"Give me a break, man," Sean said, hands in his pockets, one slim hip cocked to the side. "I'm not going to tell."

Jason and Gus looked at one another, surprised. "Okay." Jason's face lit up with a mischievous grin. "Do you want some?"

Gus started to laugh, but stopped when Sean reached out his freckled arm and grabbed the bottle.

"Why not?" With as much manliness as he could muster, Sean raised the wine bottle and began to drink.

CHAPTER 14

"What's the matter Celia, don't you feel like dancing? The band's just warming up."

Whitney — all a-flutter and with a sly look on her face — was holding Christopher's hand and grinning at Celia. Meg and Allie, who were squeezed into the corner of the back wine-tasting room with paper plates balanced on their knees, were also getting the full benefit of her show.

"I appreciate your concern, Whitney, but I'm doing just fine," Celia managed to reply, her voice shaking just a little. She couldn't believe this. After the huge fuss Whitney'd made about getting Tim to her party, she was going to be even happier if he stood Celia up.

"So glad to hear it." Whitney nuzzled against Christopher's shoulder, and he put his arm around her neck. He had his Vuarnet sunglasses on and reminded Celia of a mannequin. When the band — four middle-aged guys in sparkly red suits —

started up again, he looked away as if he was bored and snapped his fingers. Whitney projected over the music, "How about you, Meg? Did Jason go home without you?"

Meg glared, and then decided to bluff, "I really don't know, Whitney, and I really don't care."

The girls stared each other down until Meg gave in and began stacking the used punch glasses that littered the bench beside her. As she picked up one that was half full, she considered smooshing it right in Whitney's perfect face. She restrained herself, but smiled at the thought of thick, creamy pink blotting out those cold gray eyes.

"Don't you care?" Whitney said, a coy, polished fingernail to her lip. "I'd better not tell that to Jason."

Meg wondered how Celia could ever have been friends with Whitney, even for those three short weeks freshman year. In that green velvet dress, Whitney reminded Meg of the worms that came up on her lawn after a heavy rain.

Meg also wondered where exactly Jason was. He'd been so glad to see her, and she was under the impression that this was sort of a date. But now Jason had completely vanished. Allie said she'd spotted him out back with Gus and Sean when she'd gone to the bathroom. But when Meg went out to look, there was no one there, and on her way back, she'd seen Nick's Rabbit pulling into the parking lot. That had confused her so much that she'd rushed back in. Since then she hadn't seen Jason at all. Or Nick. Or Sean, for that matter.

"Well." Whitney giggled. "I'm happy that you could come, and I hope you're having a wonderful time." She started to laugh, leaned her face against placid Christopher, and then pulled him out onto the dance floor, still laughing.

Laugh, thought Celia as she watched Whitney and Christopher get swallowed up by the crowd of dancers. Giggle your stupid head off. I'm going to sit right here until Tim Holt shows up and throws his arms around me, even if I have to stay here all day and night. And if he doesn't show? Celia didn't want to think about that. She couldn't. It was too hopeless and black a thought. She felt the push of tears as Allie leaned her head on her shoulder and whispered, "Cici, can we go home now? I don't feel very good."

"Not yet." Celia put her arm around Allie, the panic and hurt starting to spread throughout her body. "Don't eat any more of that junk, okay, Al?"

Allie had cleaned not only her own plate, but Meg's and Celia's as well. She was just about to eat the frosted cookie on Celia's plate, but guiltily put it down. "Okay." She looked like she was about to start crying again, and Meg leaned in from the other side.

"We'll leave pretty soon, Al," Meg promised, still searching the crowded room for a sign of Jason or Nick.

"You promise?"

Allie raised her sweet, round face to Celia, and Celia nodded. "I promise."

The words caught in Celia's throat. She was

beginning to admit to the possibility that Tim was not going to show up, and she would have to crawl out humiliated, defeated, and stood up. Maybe Whitney was right. Maybe she was just a flirt, a piece of fluff that guys could only be interested in for ten minutes before they saw the lack of quality under the surface. Maybe Tim had been giving her messages all week that he was dumping her — don't meet me after the game, I won't pick you up for the party. Any guy who said he had to study as much as Tim this weekend had to be hiding something.

But what about when they'd sat in the car together? The way he'd kissed her and listened to her talk about her mother and told her about things that were important to him. The thought of that being a sham made the room spin and the music pound painfully in her head. It made her feel like she would never be able to trust anything in her life again.

Feeling swallowed up by the crowd and the music and the fear in her own heart, Celia huddled even closer to Meg and Allie, prayed, and kept on waiting.

At the same time, out in the field behind the winery and hidden by the tall grass, Jason stood the second bottle end up and chugged the last drops of ruby-red liquid.

"Boy," Sean said, "you sure must be used to drinking this stuff."

Jason almost spit it out, but managed to control himself. Instead he rolled over on his back, pushing down some of the soft green grass underneath him, and winked at Gus, who was snickering. It was perfect. Their little secret. It wasn't real wine they were drinking; it was vintage grape juice. They'd figured it out before they'd left the back of the winery and hiked up here, and Sean didn't have a clue. It was one of the best things Jason'd gotten away with yet. This was hysterical.

"Wow, is my head spinning," Jason mumbled in the most incoherent speech he could muster.

"Yeah?" Sean said. He closed his eyes, trying to identify this new, illicit feeling. He wasn't quite spinning yet, but he was sure he would start soon. "I think mine is, too. That last drink really did it to me."

"Nah," Gus growled, looking slightly cross-eyed. "You're not drunk."

Sean put his finger in front of his nose and tried to touch it like he'd seen the police do to drunk drivers. Sure enough, when he brought the finger to his face, he missed his nose by half an inch. "I am drunk," Sean said in a whispery voice. "It's really weird, too. You know something. . . ." He hesitated, wondering if he should trust them with this information. "I've never been drunk before."

The other two boys burst out laughing, and Sean stared at them, wondering for a minute if they were laughing at him. No . . . it was simply a matter of them being drunk, too. They'd chugged two entire bottles among the three of them, and he'd seen Jason and Gus match him swallow for swallow. Not sure quite what else to do, Sean laughed. Pretty soon all three of them were howling like wolves, rolling around on the grass, and holding their sides.

"You're a great drunk, Sean," Jason said with a sentimental streak in his voice. "The best."

"You're not bad yourself."

"I'll get blasted with you anytime."

"Me, too," Gus agreed, then sputtered out with a big laugh.

Sean sat up straighter and tried to control his long limbs. But he was still laughing so hard, and suddenly he *was* a tiny bit light-headed. He tried to be quiet, so one of the adults wouldn't hike over and catch them, but every time Jason let go with that hyena shriek of his, Sean laughed, too. Somehow, sharing this experience with these guys made him think he'd judged them too harshly. Maybe it was possible for him even to be friends with a hulk like Gus. Maybe that was part of Sean's problem. He was too intolerant, too demanding of other people. Maybe his smartness had made him stuck up.

"I'm sorry I didn't help Tim," Sean slurred graciously. "No hard feelings, okay?"

"Nahhhhh."

"If you want, I'll call him tonight and see if I can still do something."

Jason was on the ground, swaying from side to side as he stared up at the afternoon sky. "It's okay. He's taken care of."

Sean flopped over onto his stomach. He was aware of that swaying feeling, too. "You found somebody else to tutor him?"

"You could say that." Jason exploded, and he and Gus started to roar again.

149

"We have to win the championship."

"Yeah," Gus gasped, doubled over. "If we do that, we might all get blasted again!"

There were more shrieks as all three of the boys scooted like bugs having fits across the grass. Finally they caught their breaths. "You know something," Sean admitted. "I never would have thought that a party by Whitney-the-pain would be where I'd get drunk for the first time in my life."

"We never would have guessed it, either."

"Hey, you guys," Sean said, stretching out his lanky body and sitting up, "I'm going to try and walk."

Sean wobbled to his feet. He thought he could do it even though the grass did seem greener, the breeze breezier, the sky bluer, and the voices floating from the party below so much more distinct. He'd never expected he could be drunk and his senses would be so sharp. His legs were doing pretty well, too. He took three or four steps. "Wow," he said.

"Double wow," Jason echoed. He got up and walked, too, listing from side to side much more wildly than Sean. Suddenly Gus put a leg out and tripped them both. They fell back down in the grass, guffawing some more and kicking the ground. Now Sean really did feel dizzy all of a sudden. Oh, no. He was afraid it was coming. The barfing he'd always heard about. His stomach didn't feel sick at all, but they said that was when it hit you — just when you thought you were okay.

"Uh-oh," Jason worried, "you're not going to puke are you?"

"I don't know," Sean said in a tremulous voice.

"Maybe you'd just better lay down on your back and rest a minute," Gus said quietly.

"Okay."

"It's pretty intense the first time."

"Yeah."

Sean did exactly as they suggested, spreading out full-eagle on the lawn and looking up at the puffy clouds that were whipping by. A few seagulls were circling in from the ocean, and some flies were buzzing and cutting sharp corners. Now, this was a good feeling again. Very good. This was a feeling to put on tape and play back whenever things got tough.

Suddenly Sean heard footsteps swishing toward them, separating the grass. They all scrambled to sit up and see who it was.

"Hey, Sean, is that you?"

Nick's voice. Sean started laughing again and covered his face with his hands. Gus and Jason sat up soberly as if they were waiting to see what was going to happen.

Nick appeared, looming over Sean, looking like a ranch hand in his Levi's and jeans jacket. With his fists in his pockets he peered down, confused. "What are you guys doing out here?"

Sean was still laughing, although he noticed that this time Gus and Jason didn't join him. Sean grabbed one of the empty bottles and shoved it up at Nick. "What does it look like? We're drunk."

Nick's face went hot, and his eyes looked like they caught fire as he looked from Jason to Gus. Sean couldn't believe how mad he looked over such a dumb little stunt. Maybe Nick didn't think Sean had it in him to get drunk.

Nick swooped down next to Jason and grabbed his shirt. "Was this another one of your brilliant ideas, Sandy?"

Sean sat up, too, embarrassed. Nick could really be an overbearing jerk sometimes. "Nick, it's not such a big deal."

Gus was on his feet, pushing back his sleeves, like he was ready for a fight. Sean was amazed how quickly Gus had regained his balance.

"Are you guys trying to make sure that everybody at Redwood stoops to your level?" Nick accused, his face so red Sean was afraid he might burst.

"Don't get so upset, Rhodes." He smiled. It was his old, charming, teddy-bear smile, and something about the steadiness of it turned a screw inside Sean's stomach. "It's just a joke."

"What?"

Now Gus was laughing again. Only it wasn't his drunken shriek, it was the dull, dumb laugh Sean was used to hearing from him at school. Jason fished the other empty bottle out of the grass and held it up. "A joke. Look."

Gus and Jason stood cockily with their hands on their hips while Nick examined the bottle. At the same time, Sean took his bottle and for the first time read the label. It had the name of the Hain vineyard on it, a picture of the farm drawn on, and it said it was Cabernet Sauvignon, whatever that meant. But on the bottom in big bold letters Sean also made out GOURMET GRAPE JUICE. *Contains No Alcohol.*

Sean let the bottle roll back into the grass and suddenly everything *did* go topsy-turvy. They hadn't been drinking wine. They'd been drinking grape juice. He wasn't drunk — he was just a nerd, a geek. . . . Jason and Gus had made him look like a total fool. He couldn't look any of them in the face. He pitched the bottle across the field and took off back toward the winery.

Nick stayed behind and stared at Jason and Gus. Gus looked a little embarrassed, but Jason just stood there with his thumbs stuck in his suspenders like he'd just done the funniest thing in the world.

"So, what'd you do, convince Sean that he was getting drunk?"

Jason just kept his thumbs hooked and tipped back and forth on his heels. He looked so smug that Nick wanted to strangle him.

"He convinced himself." Jason grinned. "I just watched."

"Yeah, sure," Nick spat back. "You are an incredible sleazebag, Sandy. Do you know that?"

Jason's jaw tensed and he glared at Nick. "Come on, Gus. Let's go back to the party. Meg's probably wondering where I am." He brushed the dirt and grass off his trousers and started to go.

That did it. It was like a spring in Nick had just been uncoiled, and he went flying across the grass and grabbed Jason again. "Just leave my friends alone, Sandy! Do you hear, leave my friends alone!"

Jason held up his hands and backed up. He was clearly frightened and didn't want to tangle with Nick. "Okay. Okay. Don't get upset." He headed in the other direction, toward the parking lot. "Tell Meg I left. I'll see her at school. Let's go, Gus."

His head pounding and his body shaking like a paper fan, Nick watched Gus and Jason retreat. When he was a freshman he'd sat by and watched his friends get taken advantage of, hurt, almost ripped apart. He'd sworn to himself then that he'd never sit by and let that happen again. But he didn't think it would ever get as complicated as this. Confused and weary, he slumped down in the grass and put his head in his hands.

Sean went back to the party only to pick up his jacket. He stared straight ahead of him, so angry and humiliated that his teeth were clenched and his head throbbed.

How could anyone so smart be so dumb, he kept thinking. And what did smartness matter, when you could be humiliated by guys who were stupid and nasty and only a year older than you were? Sophomores were supposed to be immune to this kind of stuff, weren't they? Maybe not. Maybe being laughed at was going to be the story of his life. No. NO! Something had to change.

He quickly found his parka. It was just where he'd left it, on a bench by the door — alone, ignored. He swept it up and hurried to the main exit. People were just starting to filter out. The guy in the green shorts was still there, opening car doors and escorting the women, many of whom were wobbling in their high heels and talking too loudly, still holding wine glasses as they waited for their cars. Sean couldn't stand watching them and rudely pushed his way down the steps.

He hesitated at the bottom, taking a moment to decide between the back shortcut and the main road. Then he saw Meg, Celia, and Allie huddled together only a few yards away, backed against a ivy-covered trellis and a huge poster of Whitney's father sniffing a glass of wine. Before he could sneak off, the girls spotted him.

"Sean!" Meg called harshly.

Sean stopped but did not turn back to look at them.

"Sean, can you call one of your folks to come get us?" Meg asked in her most efficient voice. "My phone's busy, Celia's mom has a date, and Allie's folks can't come." She walked over to him. "Celia and Allie are both upset. I don't want them to have to walk all the way home. Come on, Sean. We need your help."

Of course. Celia and Allie's woes were of upmost importance, but nobody gave a second thought to how Sean had spent this wonderful party. He started to walk away.

Meg followed. "Sean! They're both having a terrible time. I don't know where Jason went. Can't you just call your mom and dad and see if they'll come get us?"

"Nick's here," he growled. "Why don't you ask him?"

Meg flinched, then pretended that it hadn't occurred to her to find Nick. "Okay, I will. I didn't know he was here," she stumbled, obviously backtracking. "But in the meantime, can you just call your folks?"

Allie and Celia rushed over, too. "Sean, please," Allie pleaded. She looked so pathetic, she reminded Sean of those big-eyed kids in the paintings people sold out of their cars on Redwood Boulevard.

"Please," Celia reinforced, "we know you don't know what's going on, but can't you just call anyway?"

"I don't know what's going on?" Sean turned on them and argued. *"I don't know what's going on? How come if I'm so smart you act like I'm so stupid! And how come I act like I'm so stupid when I'm supposed to be so smart?"*

The girls stared at him, amazed. In all the years they'd known each other they'd never seen Sean blow up like this. A few older people turned around to look, but Sean paid no attention.

"You think I don't know what's going on?" he continued in a softer, but even more intense voice. "Well, maybe I'll just tell you a few of the things I do know. I do know that Allie was too much of a wimp to really work on our project, and then she blames me when I drop it. And now she acts like it's my fault she broke up with L.P." He faced Meg. "I know you and Nick don't have any idea what you feel about each other, so you go around avoiding each other and acting like jerks so you won't have to find out."

"Sean — "

Sean cut Meg off and pointed at Celia. "And I know that you don't care enough about Tim to

156

even find out why he's not at this stupid party. All you care about is that he shows up and is the big basketball star so you can impress Whitney Hain!!!"

Quiet. Just a few car honks, the music inside, and a drunken woman's giggle. Sean's outburst was over, and the three girls stood openmouthed as they stared at one another.

Sean tromped away. He couldn't look at them any more.

Celia was about to yell for him to come back, when she saw a tall figure frozen in the shadows, not more than six feet away, just under the canopy where people pulled up in their cars. Her heart cracked in two. "Tim. How long have you been standing there?"

He stood stiffly, dressed up in a jacket and tie, the late afternoon light showing off the pain in his eyes. "Long enough."

"Tim, wait. I want to. . . ."

But he was already gone, gracefully jogging to catch up with Sean. Meg and Allie came up beside Celia and touched her, but it didn't make any difference. Celia knew in that moment that all the things she cared about before didn't matter. Not Whitney or Christopher or her mother and their crummy house. Not flirting or working in the mall or nice clothes or any of it. What mattered was Tim, and how she felt about him and how he felt about her.

And that was over now. Killed. Dead as a bug she'd just squashed under her foot. And there would be no bringing it back to life.

CHAPTER 15

"Jason left," Nick bluntly told Meg. She was still standing out in front of the winery with Allie and Celia, the three of them looking like homeless wanderers waiting for a train. "He told me to tell you."

Meg whipped around to face him, her dark hair flying. She was clearly already angry about something and was now sending the force of her frustration at Nick. "Where did he go?" she demanded. "Why are *you* telling me?"

Nick backed up to let a group of well-dressed older people pass. The party was really breaking up now, and it seemed like the entire Hain staff was gathered on the front steps to say good-bye. It was a terrible place to have an important conversation. He tried to move closer to Meg, but she kept her distance. "He and I had kind of an argument. I thought it was better if he just went home."

"You thought it was better?"

"Yeah. I told him to go."

"*You* told him to go?" she repeated, her voice rising and her eyes getting big. "What right did you have to tell him anything about me?" Nick could tell that if there weren't so many people around she might start yelling at him, but they had to put on phony smiles and move out of the way and pretend that they were having a grand old time.

"It's okay. I'll take you all home," Nick announced leading the way to the parking lot. Celia and Allie were quick to follow. Meg stood behind with her arms folded across her blazer, glaring at Nick, until she realized it was getting late and she had no choice, so she joined them. She climbed in the front seat, slammed the door, then sat with her back to him and her face against the window.

Nick drove. It was hard to see because dusk was just starting to fall, or maybe it was that his brain felt so blurry and tired. He tried to concentrate on the road as they left the vineyards, the big old houses, and the open fields, and headed toward the more cluttered, orderly neighborhoods of downtown. It was so quiet he felt like a chauffeur, except for the angry huffs from Meg next to him, and the occasional sniffs from Allie in the back.

It was a good thing he'd gone on this route a hundred million times with his parents, because his head was so filled with Meg and Jason and Tim and Sean that he might not have been able to find his way. On automatic pilot, he somehow found Celia's house and pulled up. Her windows were dark, but Meg's were lit up next door, and Sean's parents were across the street loading something into the van they used for their bicycle shop. When they saw Nick, they smiled and waved. Nick gulped, then waved back. He noticed that none of the girls raised a hand.

Meg shoved her shoulder against the door and got out, not even bothering to hold the seat for Celia and Allie.

"I'm getting out here, too," Allie told him. As if he was disappointed that he didn't get to drive her back over to their neighborhood.

"Fine," he said.

"Thanks," Celia said, and they scrambled to catch up with Meg, who was already on her own lawn.

Nick couldn't stand any more. He was trying to handle this like a mature person, but he was still going like a rocket inside, ready to shoot out of his seat, he was so angry and confused and frustrated. He watched Meg's leggy stance and knew she was making a point of not turning back to look at him, as if it were his fault that she was involved with a jerk who didn't even flinch at the idea of not driving her home. It was like the way she'd made a point of sitting as far away from Nick as she could in the car. As if he would contaminate her by bumping her with his shoulder or his knee. But he only had to think of Sean . . . or that girl with the broken ankle last fall . . . or Tim Holt to know that he had to warn Meg about Jason Sandy. No matter what his own feelings were — and what were they? — he had to get through to her before it was too late.

"Meg!!!" he hollered, lifting himself so he was halfway out his open window.

All three girls turned back to stare. Even from two houses away, he could see the deep sadness in Celia's eyes and the puffy redness in Allie's. He only had to imagine Sean standing next to them and the picture would have been complete.

Meg shifted, as if she was deciding whether or not to even acknowledge his call. Then she whispered something to the other girls and pointed them up toward her porch. Arm in arm, Allie and Celia went up Meg's walkway, past the planters and the pots and the old-fashioned swing, until Meg's mother let them into the house. Meg arrogantly walked back to the car. Her hands were on her slim hips and her long hair hid almost half her face.

"What?"

"Get in."

"Why?"

"I have to talk to you."

"About what?"

"Come on, Meg. Just get in."

It was like convincing her to take a ride with a criminal. Why couldn't they be easy and natural with each other like they used to be? Maybe he should just jump out of the car and tackle her to the ground or challenge her to a foot race like when they were kids — loser has to listen to anything the winner wants to say and admit that he's right. That made more sense than what had been going on between them since New Year's.

Finally Meg got in but sat defiantly with her back flat against the door, her feet on the seat, and her arms around her knees.

Now Nick wasn't sure how to begin. Jason isn't good enough for you, he considered. No. Well, you see Meg, Jason's kind of screwed up. Uh-unh. That wasn't definite enough. How about, Sandy's a total sleaze, and if you hang out with him one more day you're as big a jerk as he is! Stalling for time, Nick started the engine.

"Where are we going?" Meg demanded, again like he was kidnapping her or something.

"Everybody's watching here," Nick said quickly. "I can't handle it." Sure enough, when he pulled away from the curb, Meg saw Allie and Celia spying on them through the McCall's living room curtains. He drove about three blocks, finally pulling over in front of an ice-cream parlor on the edge of downtown. He turned off the ignition, and the car rumbled a few times.

Meg looked up at him, her mouth in almost a pout and her blue eyes defensive as anything.

"What right did you have to tell Jason to go home without me?" she said, surprising him by starting the conversation.

Nick took a deep breath. Now came the hard part, figuring out exactly how much to tell her. He knew it would be easy if he simply spilled the whole truth. But then what? Sean would be twice as humiliated if the girls knew how he'd been duped — and if he told Meg, of course the others would know, too. And Tim. That was even tougher. Even though Nick would never take part in a cheating scheme, some weird code of honor told him not to rat or spread it around. Somehow it would seem even more unfair if Tim got caught and punished for something that wasn't even his idea. So now that Nick had Meg as a captive audience, he didn't know what to say.

"I asked you a question. What business of yours is it if Jason drives me home or not?"

Nick was overwhelmed with confusion. Part of him wanted to yell at Meg, to tell her she was being a stupid jerk, while another part of him kept staring at her hair and her eyes and the way her mouth was quivering in the corners and he wanted to hold her to. . . . Sometimes he had these feelings for Meg that were stronger than anything he'd ever known, and it made him crazy. She was the girl he'd grown up with, after all. You weren't supposed to have feelings like this about the girl you'd collected bugs with and had helped make tents out of lawn chairs and old sheets. He tried not to look at her and went back to the subject of Jason.

"I can't explain it all, but Jason is not a good person, Meg."

"Why?"

"I told you, I can't explain it. He's just not honest. He doesn't care how he hurts people as long as he can have a good time."

"What do you mean?"

"Just take my word for it, okay?"

"No. That's not okay. Give me an example."

"All right! Like . . . like that time last year when he broke that girl's ankle during the game. . . ."

"If you tell me one more time about that girl

and her stupid ankle, I'm going to scream. You know what I think, Nick?"

"What?"

"I think you just don't like seeing me with any guy who isn't Mr. Boring. It's like I'm your sister or something and you have to protect me, even though you don't have any idea how I really feel!"

She was pointing her finger at him, and he grabbed her hand. "That's not true," he said, caught up in the heat of things and the sudden nearness of her face.

"WELL, THEN WHAT IS?"

Nick wasn't sure what made him do it, but he suddenly couldn't hold himself back. Her face was so close, her skin so soft but reddening from her anger, her hair so silky and . . . his hand grabbed her shoulder and before he even realized he was really doing it, he was kissing her. For one second she seemed to melt into him, and it was so right, so perfect that the argument, the car, Tim and Jason and Sean, the entire world disappeared. It was only the two of them. He pulled back to catch his breath, his heart was pounding so hard he was dizzy, and he started to kiss her again.

But she pushed him away with the flat of both hands, so hard it knocked the wind out of him. She was crying.

"That's not funny!" she heaved, the tears spilling down her cheeks. She brought a hand to her mouth. "What is this? Just another way to prove that I'm not supposed to have a boyfriend in this school like everybody else?" She was sobbing now, and her voice came out in awful gasps and starts. "That I'm supposed to be dull, dependable Meg McCall, who sits around waiting for you to ignore me so I can make dips for your parties and be there when you think you might want me around. Well, forget it, Nick. That Meg doesn't exist anymore! Maybe last year I would have fallen for this, but not now."

Nick's head was still reeling from the kiss. He just wanted her to calm down, to come back into his arms, to stop crying and yelling, and to take away the painful ache her tears put in his chest. "Meg — "

"I don't want to hear it," she cried, getting out of the car. "I won't let you make fun of me, and I don't believe anything you say or do. You're wrong about Jason and I know it. And I'm going to still see him, and if you don't like it, that's just tough!"

Then he heard her hightops slapping against the sidewalk as she ran full speed down the street.

By that night all three girls were cried out. They sat on Meg's lawn, bundled up in blankets and the old sleeping bag with hounds and birds printed on the inside, and stared, shoulder to shoulder to shoulder, at the endless dark sky.

"Do you think Sean was right?" Allie asked softly, her curls drooping over her forehead so a few almost touched the mascara smudged under her eyes.

Celia frowned. She sat in the middle, temporarily taking over Meg's usual role as comforter and leader. "About what?"

"That I'm a wimp. That I didn't work on the

project at all. That I don't really work hard at anything." She pulled the open sleeping bag up over her soft shoulders. "That's what L.P. thinks."

"I don't know, Al," soothed Celia.

"Maybe I should go in there and do that computer art thing all by myself. Just to show them. What do you think?"

"Don't do it just to show them," Celia advised sadly. "It's dumb to do things just to prove something to other people." Her voice caught a little at the end of her sentence, and Allie looked at her. "If you want to do it, then do it. But not to impress somebody else."

At last Meg stirred. She'd been so quiet since she'd come back from the ride with Nick, so unlike her normal together self that it had scared Celia and Allie. "I wonder if that's it," she said, so softly the others could barely hear her.

"What?"

"Nothing."

Was that it? Meg wondered. Was she trying to prove something, to impress Nick with her wild boyfriend, with the fact that she wasn't going to be Miss Dependable, Miss School Spirit and A for Attitude? Did everything still center around Nick?

She had no reason to believe that Jason was a creep. Sure, he was a little careless, but he was also quick and funny, and he did stand up to Whitney and make them all laugh. So maybe it was Nick who had the problem.

Nick. Thinking back on his kiss made her head whirl, but it was mixed with so much fear and doubt and pain that she tried not to think about it. She would concentrate on Jason for now. She'd find out if he was a good guy or not. And if he was, she'd stick with him no matter what Nick said.

Allie reached over and touched Meg's hand, cutting into her contemplation.

"Do you think sophomore year is this weird for everybody?" she asked.

The three girls looked at one another.

"I don't know, Al," Meg sighed. "I just don't know."

CHAPTER
16

Almost overnight winter came to Redwood Hills, but there wasn't a single snowman or frozen pond. Instead there came rain. Cold, heavy rain that streaked into the ground in wind-blown slants and made swimming pools overflow, gutters spill, and turned every hillside into a mass of mud that threatened to weaken and slide. It was almost as if Redwood Hills had forgotten it was part of the state of California. The weather became the front-page news all over town. But on Thursday, when Meg, Celia, and Allie met in front of the main office near the flagpole, they were trying to forget about the rain. It wasn't easy, water was pouring off the eaves and it sounded like they were standing in a shower, but they persisted. Allie was almost invisible in a huge army-green trench coat and her black hat. Meg wore only a rain slicker over her jeans and didn't seem to care that her hair was dripping, while Celia carefully shook out her umbrella, then checked her face in a pocket mirror.

They'd all stayed after school for separate missions — Meg to give her treasurer's report at the sophomore council meeting, Allie to take a make-up test for Spanish, and Celia to try and talk to Tim. It was that task that all the girls agreed was the most urgent.

"Any luck?" Meg asked Celia as she peered back along the hallways and then out at the parking lot. Their friend Maria Martinez was supposed to give them all a ride home after she finished her debate club meeting. Meg tried to pick out Maria's station wagon, but the solid sheet of water made everything a blur.

Celia wrapped her raincoat more tightly around herself. Everything in her life felt cold. "I sat there for almost the whole practice, and Tim wouldn't even look at me."

"Maybe he was just concentrating," Allie offered glumly, her hat pulled down almost over her eyes. "The game tomorrow night is really important."

"I don't think so. Jason dropped by, and Tim didn't have any trouble talking to him." Even before Celia had finished telling Allie, she remembered that Tim and Jason and Gus had chatted through the whole break, off in the corner, whispering as if they were discussing state secrets. They were probably hiding from her. When the practice was finally over, and she'd worked up her nerve to walk up to Tim and make him talk to her, he brushed her off by saying he was going to Cotter Valley to coach his kids and had to leave that second. Celia was used to walking away from boys without a care, not having them ditch her with half her heart on the floor. "Nick was being weird, too," she said absently, as if the whole world had gone off kilter.

Meg tensed. "What do you mean?"

Celia stared out at the rain. "He wasn't talking to anybody. When they took the break and Jason was there, Nick just kept throwing free throws over and over like his life depended on it. It was really bizarre."

Nobody said anything after that. It was too hard to know what to say without sounding overly sensitive or disappointed or hurt, so instead they stood there listening to the rain. Finally Meg splashed her running shoe down. "Where is Maria?" she mentioned impatiently.

"She's late."

"I know, Al."

"Well you don't have to be so crabby. Hey, guess who I ran into today?" Allie said.

"Sean?"

Allie shook her head. "I always run into him, but it's getting so I don't think it even matters. In Thorson's class now he pretends like he's too busy to talk to me, and then as soon as the bell rings he leaves really fast. I think he's been going in there at lunch time, too, this week."

"Probably."

"But that's not who I meant that I ran into." Allie stepped away from the wall and faced them, her books clutched to her chest. "I saw L.P."

"You did?"

"What happened?"

170

Both girls craned over their notebooks, looking as if they hoped Allie had good news about L.P. and that it might rub off on them.

"I was going to gym last period, and I ran across the quad because I was late," Allie explained. "He was coming the other way, and we both stopped in the middle of the quad and stood there in the pouring rain not saying anything. It seemed like forever. Then finally he asked me how I was and I said I was okay and we stood there some more until the bell rang. He left, and I went to the bathroom and cried for about ten minutes and was really late for gym."

"Did you get in trouble?"

Allie smiled. "No. We were supposed to have swimming today. Can you believe that? Because of all the rain, by the time I got there, Miss Snyder was still trying to figure out where we were supposed to go instead. We ended up playing jacks in the locker room. Snyder is this amazing jacks player."

The conversation ceased as they all stared out at the rain again.

"Are you sure Maria's coming?" Allie said finally.

"She told me if she was late to go find her in the debate room. Maybe we should start over there."

"Okay."

Meg led the way and Allie followed, but Celia stayed put, mesmerized by something she saw on the street out front. . . . The city bus stopping at the corner right in front of Redwood High. The bus that Celia had taken to ballet lessons or over to Nick's and Allie's when she was younger. Also the same bus that went past the hilly section of Redwood, through the vineyards and the ranches, and over to Cotter Valley.

Celia didn't know why, but all of a sudden she ran. The rain hit her face and dripped down the back of her neck, but she kept running, yelling for the driver to wait, and waving like a crazy person.

The bus stopped and then amid a cloud of steam and exhaust, the door whooshed back open, and the driver winked.

"You just made it," he grinned.

Celia hopped on, then turned back and yelled to Meg and Allie, *"Go on home without me! I'll talk to you later."*

Their confused faces became a wet blur as the bus jerked into motion and Celia dropped her fare in the box. She fell back into the front seat. She had it all to herself, and she pressed her face to the window, watching downtown turn to open land and rows of grapevines. Finally she leaned forward. "Do you know where the YMCA is in Cotter Valley?" she asked the driver projecting over the *thwick-thwack* of the windshield wipers.

"Sure, I can show you."

"Thanks."

Celia watched some more of the scenery go by, then sat back with her heart suddenly going like those wipers, because she knew what she was doing was probably insane. Trying to talk to Tim again seemed hopeless and really asking for it. Still, she stayed in her seat, resisting the impulse to get off early, even when she saw a bus stop across the street and head back in the opposite direction.

Twenty minutes later, the driver peered around and nodded to her. "That's it," he told her, opening the door and pointing at a plain brick building across the street.

"Thank you."

Celia smiled at the driver, then she hopped down the three short steps until she touched the street corner. Immediately she noticed the rain was finally letting up, and she wouldn't have to bother with her umbrella. Instead she just swung her arms out like she was starting a hike, and then crossed the street, where she found the steps to the old Y. Up she went, and then she pushed open the door. Instantly she breathed dust and old wood, and somewhere in the distance she heard the thump of a basketball. She passed a desk and a bulletin board covered with notices. No one was around, and she kept on going. She went through another set of doors and the echoey sound got louder.

"Hey, Billy, that's it. You got it. Hook that ball right over your head. Thatta boy."

Celia stopped. There he was, standing at one end of the gym, watching his kids run up to the basket and shoot. He had a big smile on his face, and he looked more relaxed than Celia had ever seen him.

"That's it!!" Tim cheered, clapping his hands. He ran over to collect the ball and, laughing, faked handing it to one of the older boys. Instead he passed it to the littlest kid there.

Celia stood quietly and watched. Now Tim

was demonstrating a jump shot — his body pure grace and liquid movement — when in the middle of it, he finally spotted Celia. He came down awkwardly and the ball twanged off the rim. "What are you doing here?" he said, not looking at her, but scooping the ball up in front of him.

She took a deep breath and spoke quickly, afraid she would lose her nerve. "I just want to tell you one thing and then I'll go away. At first I did just want to be with you because you were a basketball star and I wanted to impress Whitney and her friends. But that was before I got to know you. Now I just like you for you. I don't know if you even care anymore how I feel, but I wanted you to know. That's all." She finally looked up at him. For a moment they stared at each other, until they realized that all the boys were watching them.

Tim threw the ball hard to a boy with a fuzzy crewcut. "Everybody line up and start working on free throws." The boys hustled back to the top of the key, although a few looked back occasionally at Tim and Celia.

Celia shivered. Her hair was still wet and her feet were freezing. "Anyway, that's all I wanted to say," she whispered, looking into his face again.

For a moment Tim's dark eyes softened, and Celia felt like she was floating on hope. His eyes were saying, Yes, I believe you. I care about you, too. I'm so glad you came all this way to tell me this.

"Do you really mean that?"

"Of course."

"Do you think you'd still feel that way if I didn't play tomorrow night against Napa?" His eyes locked onto hers, as if this was the most important question.

Celia was confused. Why was he suddenly talking about the game tomorrow night? What did that have to do with her and how they felt about one another? "Tim, what are you talking about? Why wouldn't you play? You're so good, and everybody's counting on you."

That was when something changed. A door slammed somewhere inside him and he turned away, his sensitive face again becoming hard and angry. "Yeah. Right. I'll play tomorrow, no matter what else happens. I'll be Tim Holt basketball star, and I won't disappoint anybody. Because if I don't play, then it doesn't matter what I do." He was backing onto the court, and Celia had no idea what he was talking about. All she knew was that they'd almost come together, almost figured something out, and then it was gone. . . .

Tim blew his whistle, and the shrill scream echoed off the walls and inside Celia's head. She knew from the sound that her chance was gone. It had been there for a moment, but then it had completely disappeared. No use waiting around for another. She had learned something, too. Win or lose, flirting had never hurt like this.

Celia turned and headed out — past the entrance, through the damp frosty air, and across the street. She sat on a wet bench to wait for the bus, the dampness seeping through her coat and her stockings. She started to shiver all over and wondered if she would ever get warm.

CHAPTER 17

"Sean, where are you, Sean?"

Allie was at school early the next morning, almost an hour before first period. Since she didn't like school normally, being there with just a few teachers, the janitors waxing the lunchroom floor, and the super-studious types, who were already in the library, really gave her the creeps. But she had to find Sean. All night she'd been thinking about him, what he'd said last Sunday, and how he was one of her best friends ever. It was bad enough to lose your boyfriend, but losing a best friend, too, was more than Allie could even think about.

It was rainy and dark as Allie poked around the empty campus checking the library, the science labs, the shop, even the gym . . . though she knew Sean didn't like gym. He preferred long bike rides or hiking in the woods. Meg had seen him riding his bike to school before seven o'clock in the morning all week long, so maybe that's where he was, pretending he was riding the Tour de France up on Capitola Mountain. But in this rain? No. Even Sean wasn't that crazy.

So Allie had one place left to look, the place she'd been avoiding because she knew she'd have to face Mr. Thorson. The dreaded computer center. It was at the other end of the school, so she had to walk across the quad. She had dressed for it — she was wearing boots, her trench coat, gloves, and had a scarf wrapped so high around her face she felt like a mummy — but still it was shivery, so she was relieved when she finally got into the hall. Once there, she saw banner after paper banner pepping everybody up for the game that evening. The Spirit Club had really done a number this time. GO GRIZZLIES. NAIL NAPA. CLAW 'EM. There was hardly an inch of bare wall. One banner, saying, NEVER AGAIN, NAPA, was draped across the ceiling and starting to fall down. Allie ducked under it and headed toward Thorson's room.

She opened the door and peaked in. Fifteen blank computer screens stared back at her, plus Thorson's bald head shining up at the front of the room. No Sean. Allie's heart sank.

"Yes, Allie?" Thorson said, before she could get away.

She stood just inside the doorway. It was still forty-five minutes before first period. "I was just looking for Sean Pendleton."

Thorson was putting on a tweed hat and a raincoat. "Haven't seen him. I'm going over to the teacher's room for some coffee. If you want, you can wait to see if he shows up."

Allie glanced around, uncomfortable at the idea of sitting in the computer center alone, but it was so early and the rain was coming down hard again. "Okay."

He gave her a strange look, as if he was just starting to wonder what his F-minus-for-attitude student was doing there before school. "Don't break anything," he said. He gave her one more puzzled look, and then he was gone.

"Don't break anything," Allie imitated in a sing-song voice. Thorson treated her like she was some dumb freshman or a juvenile delinquent who was going to smash the screens or put chewing gum in the keyboards. What kind of dope did Thorson think she was? Of course, what kind of a dope had she acted like? Since September she'd done nothing in his class but stare at the clock, and try to get away with doing as little as possible.

Trying to forget that, Allie sat down in Sean's chair and flicked on the computer. Bright green letters blinked at her, a sharp contrast to the dark morning outside. Automatically, Allie loaded the disks the way Thorson had taught them. WHERE ARE YOU SEAN? she then typed tentatively, imitating the way he'd always write her messages on the screen. PLEASE DON'T BE MAD AT ME. LET'S DO OUR PROJECT AGAIN. I THOUGHT OF A GOOD TITLE. "NERDS OF THE FUTURE MAKE FRIENDS WITH THE DINOSAURS." YOU LIKE?

She pressed the wrong key and the computer beeped at her.

178

"Oh, shut up," she grumbled. "Who asked you?"

She ran her bitten fingernails over the keys and listened to the clack, clip, clack. This room was so lonely and bare! Thorson had to keep the cleanest room in the entire school. The blackboard was all wiped off except for some printed instructions to his first-period class. The manuals were so neatly stacked on the side shelves it might have been a book store. Thorson didn't even put stuff on the walls like other teachers did. Desperate for distraction and company, Allie went back to the computer screen.

HELP! I'M BEING HELD PRISONER IN A COMPUTER CLASS.

Remembering a little of what Sean had showed her, she made a stick figure appear on the screen, then chased it with an asterisk.

THERE'S SOMEONE AFTER ME. OH, NO!! IT MUST BE THE ANTINERD SQUAD. WHERE ARE THE DINOSAURS?

She picked up the mouse, the small hand control, and drew in a small dinosaur — actually her version of a dinosaur. Sean called it an Allieosaurus Rex. She moved a leg so it almost looked like it was lumbering across the screen. She tried to remember the background they had been working on for their art piece, the way it looked like a futuristic version of the shopping mall.

"Great," Allie laughed when she saw the dinosaur's legs move. It looked pretty real, and she felt just a little tinge of excitement at seeing the possibilities for their idea. That excitement was replaced with sadness when she realized that it would never be anything more than just an idea now. One dinosaur on a screen wasn't going to do it. It would take a lot more work. The background had to be filled out, the dinosaur had to move against a futuristic shopping mall.

Allie quickly reached for the power switch. She didn't want to be reminded of what they'd almost created. It was too painful. The screen blurred, then faded, and the dinosaur disappeared.

She stared at the blank screen. It was stupid sitting in here, working on something she had no idea how to do. She couldn't possibly figure this stuff out, so she'd better do her boring history assignment, but as she flipped through her binder for her history notes, a sheet of paper from the back went scooting across the floor and Allie grabbed for it, recognizing it instantly . . . the last bit of computer program that she and Sean had been working on. It was written in BASIC and there were about fifty lines. It was the program that was supposed to make the dinosaur move while putting in a detailed background. She had explained to Sean what she had wanted it to look like, and he'd written the program explaining everything he did in that patient, clear Sean way.

Something in Allie made her reach for the switch and turn on the computer again. She'd start over. Futuristic dinosaurs were a lot more fun than looking up dates for her history homework, and parts of Sean's program *did* make sense to her. She remembered Sean telling her that each dot on the screen was represented by a number, and they were called pixels. You could do all kinds of stuff simply by manipulating the numbers. If she typed in this line he'd written down, and then ran the program. . . .

"Yes." Allie exhaled softly. Suddenly the dinosaur wasn't alone anymore. There was a big leafy tree right behind him, and it was swaying back and forth no less. Amazing. But the tree was too big, and so was the doorway next to it. In contrast they made the dinosaur look too small, and dinosaurs had to be gigantic.

Allie quickly went back to the paper. There was another line but it wasn't quite filled in. She started trying to figure out the numbers that would make it work. Of course, she wouldn't know how to do it, she told herself, but she had to get that doorway to look right. It was driving her crazy, so maybe she should give it a try. If she really thought about it and remembered all the stuff that Sean and Thorson had told her. . . . She threw open her notebook, tore out a piece of paper, and started adding and subtracting pixels.

A half hour later, Allie didn't hear a thing when Thorson walked in. She looked up and let out a little gasp of surprise as she saw his bald head towering over her. He was rubbing his chin and had a funny, amused expression.

"You're still here," he said, standing back to look at her screen.

Of course, I'm still here, what does it look like? Allie almost answered. Instead she shrugged. She was too distracted watching Thorson's face. She wanted to know what he thought of her drawing on the screen.

Thorson knelt down next to her. "That's pretty

good. Do you remember how to save it and make the computer print out the program for you?"

Allie considered bluffing, pretending she *did* know — after all they'd covered that in class already — or acting like she didn't care if she kept her work or not. But she did care! She knew she was getting somewhere, and she wanted to keep going. "No, I don't really remember," she admitted softly.

Thorson flipped through her manual and pressed it open with the heel of his hand. "I'll show you, but the instructions are right there if you forget. Okay?"

"Okay."

He patiently showed her the commands. It was a lot less complicated than figuring out the little dots on the screen. Thorson quickly hooked up the printer, and a minute later Allie held a piece of paper covered with numbers.

She stared at it.

Thorson tapped her as kids started to file in. "Allie, what do you have first period?"

"Huh?" Allie looked up, still fascinated.

He was almost smiling. "First period. You remember, Redwood High, 1986, planet Earth."

"Oh. Um, Spanish. Mrs. Balfour."

"Well, don't you think you'd better go?"

"Huh? Oh, yeah." She looked out the window. The rain had let up a little, and the hall was packed with students. They were yelling, and two seniors were running through the crowd, playing football with someone's lunch. She quickly stowed the paper and put on her coat. "I guess so."

Now Thorson was leaning back against the

182

heater, staring at her with folded arms. He was really smiling. "See you fourth period."

Allie turned around in the doorway. "Yeah." She waved. "See you in fourth!"

"JASON!!!!" Meg screamed four periods later. She was on her way to lunch and hollered so loudly that her voice felt like it was breaking in half. She jumped over puddles like a hurdler, stretching her long, pretty legs, then she made her feet move like lightning. "JASON!! Wait up!!!"

He was at the gate that led to the gym and stopped for a second, looking back so that Meg was sure he'd heard her. Meg took a short cut over the corner of the baseball diamond, but when she finally caught up with Jason, she was panting and her rain slicker felt oppressively hot and close. She ripped open the front snaps, grinned, and bumped him with her elbow.

"Hi, deaf man," she teased.

"Hi." He kept on walking, his eyes almost glazed, arms stiff.

Meg walked alongside, imitating his tense posture. The intensity of his movement reminded her of Groucho Marx and made her giggle. She mimed tipping the ash off a cigar. "So what's up with tonight?" she said in her best Groucho imitation, which was pretty terrible. "Do we still have a hot date for after this game? Are we going to make Napa beg for mercy?"

Jason didn't pick up on her joke, which for Jason was very unusual. Especially since all week they'd been getting along well — he'd stuck funny notes in her locker, teased her so much during lunch there'd almost been a major food fight, even kissed her again Wednesday after school. She'd found that thinking about Nick now was so confusing that she'd blocked his comments about Jason out of her mind. She hadn't even brought up the misunderstanding about driving home after Whitney's party.

"Meg, I'm in a hurry," Jason said with a gruffness she'd never heard before. His face looked older, his big eyes almost squinched shut with worry.

"Why? What's up?" It was obvious now that Jason wasn't kidding around.

He held a couple of pieces of notebook paper in one fist and muttered under his breath. "I don't believe he'd do this. What an idiot. What an idiot!"

Meg didn't say anything else. Jason was so caught up in whatever he was doing that he barely noticed her as she trailed after him. When they entered the gym, Meg stayed in the doorway, sure that Jason was headed for the guys' locker room. But he went past the locker room door and began to run, the tails of his sweater flying, his arms chugging like crazy. When he got to Coach Boyd's office, he stopped in front of the closed door. Curious, Meg slowly made her way down the hall and watched him.

Jason put his ear against Boyd's door and listened until a look of pure agony passed over his face and he jumped back, fist raised, and pounded the opposite wall.

"That jerk! This is terrible, terrible." Meg could hear him curse as she got closer.

Her first instinct was to comfort him, to find out what was wrong and make it go away, but before she could make a move, Boyd's door swung open, and the coach walked out. Coach Boyd wasn't alone; Tim Holt was with him.

Tim looked like he had just lost the game of his life. Boyd patted Tim once on the shoulder, then made an angry U-turn, and walked back in Meg's direction.

Meg pretended to take a drink from the fountain as Boyd passed, then slipped behind the half door at the entrance to the equipment room in time to see the coach's face. Boyd looked as wigged out as Tim and Jason. He was holding his forehead with one hand and sighing so loudly he sounded like a bicycle pump. From the back he looked slumped, old, and tired. After he left, Meg stood quietly by the equipment room and waited. She had to know what was going on.

Jason was holding the papers in his fist, pushing them up into Tim's face as if they were proof of some terrible crime. "Why didn't you take these from Roger Sandler?"

Tim stared off into the gym, his long, lean body looking oddly breakable and full of sadness. "I appreciate your trying to help, Jason," he said in a shaky voice. "But I couldn't do it."

Jason hopped from foot to foot, almost like he was dribbling a basketball himself. "So you passed the test on your own, right?"

"I didn't take it. I told Kitzen I wasn't following the stuff on it, and she said she'd let me get tutored and make it up later."

"Yeah? So?"

"So what."

"SO WHAT ABOUT THE TEAM?"

"I'm off."

"What?"

"I'm off the team. For now."

"You're off? YOU'RE OFF? I went to all that trouble to help you, and you're off because you didn't even try and pass the test?"

"I couldn't do it, Jason."

"You couldn't do it?" Jason repeated in a nasty growl. He looked around to see if anyone was near, either not noticing Meg or not caring that she was the only one. "YOU COULDN'T DO IT?" Jason pummeled the air with his fists and jumped like he was doing a war dance.

"I'm not a cheater," Tim came back, his eyes wide, his chin thrust forward.

"Do you think I went to all this trouble so you could think about whether or not you were a cheater?" Jason backed up and paced the hall. "Listen, Holt, it was very simple. I got Sandler to give you a copy of the answers, you memorize them and take the stupid test, and then you play basketball for your school." He held up the papers again, which Meg realized were Roger's answers, then crumpled them up and threw them on the ground. "It's not my fault you're too stupid to pass your math class and stay on the team yourself." He looked like he wanted to punch Tim, but he was too small. Instead he pointed a threatening finger. "Man, you make me sick."

186

"What was I supposed to do?" Tim shouted, finally exploding. "So I pass this test; GREAT! Then what about the next one and the one after that? Do I just keep getting Sandler's answers and writing them on my sleeve? Do I do that senior year, too? And when I go to college? Jason, I thought you were a friend."

Jason laughed. It was a mean, hollow laugh that made Meg ache. "Yeah. Friends help each other out, don't they? A *friend* doesn't do things to make his buddies look stupid, like letting his team lose when his *buddy* has been out there pumping up this school for the entire year. I don't get you, Holt," Jason said disgustedly. "I can't believe you'd give up playing ball for this. I can't wait until people hear how you let yourself get thrown off the team. Because you know something, Holt? Nobody cares about you and your honesty in your idiot math class. All anybody cares about is that you make this school win. And if you can't do that, you're nothing. Do you hear me? NOTHING!"

Tim's whole body tensed, as if he had been hit with a bucket of ice water. He tried his best not to show how he had been stunned. Jason stomped his foot, and then turned around. He headed toward Meg. When she stepped out to intercept him, she wasn't sure whether he knew she'd been listening or not, but she held her ground and their eyes met.

"Well?" Jason said angrily.

Meg couldn't say anything for a moment. She felt like her head might burst.

"It wasn't my fault," Jason persisted.

187

Meg couldn't believe that Jason had it so wrong. She wasn't angry because of Tim. She was angry because of Jason and his scheme. Finally she managed to stammer it out. "So you were going to help Tim cheat," she said abruptly.

"It wasn't cheating," Jason scowled. "We were just going to help him with his stupid test. He's going to be sorry now he didn't take us up on the offer."

Meg wanted to shake Jason. His big brown eyes no longer made her think of puppies or teddy bears; they were the eyes of someone who never looked at one thing long enough to know what it was worth. Nick's words replayed in her head — Sandy is not a good person, he's not honest. He might be fun, but you can't trust him, she added to the list.

"So what's going to happen now?" Meg demanded.

Jason angrily turned the fountain handle and took a drink. "He'll flunk and we'll lose." He waved an angry hand. "Who cares about him? I'll figure out something else."

"I thought you were his friend."

"Who can be friends after a guy does that to you?"

Meg now felt a little stupid. She flashed on Nick's warning again, how all along he'd known that Jason was not the boy for her. She suddenly found herself remembering Nick's kiss and her head felt so fuzzy that the hallway was like a spinning tunnel.

Jason's angry voice brought her back. "So I'll meet you after the game tonight?"

She stared right at him, determined to regain her balance. "I don't think so."

The slightest flicker of hurt passed over his face, like a single frame in a full-length movie. Then he smiled and looked beyond her to the next conquest and good time, wherever it was to be.

"Okay with me," he spat out, his eyes still unseeing. "I have a feeling it's not going to be a very good game anyway."

CHAPTER 18

"Hey, look over there. Is that who I think it is?"

"It can't be."

"It is, I'm sure. Is he hurt? Why isn't he playing?"

"Oh, no. We're in trouble if he's not in the game."

The pointed fingers, the whispers, the nudges began to pass from person to person and row to row.

"You know what I heard on the bus coming over here?"

"What?"

"Well, I don't know if it's true, but Rebecca Steinmetz — you know, the blonde cheerleader — she told Jennifer, my friend in the band. . . ."

"About Tim Holt? Really?"

"Then he's off the team?"

"I'm not totally sure, but I heard. . . ."

"Is that why he's sitting in the stands all by himself?"

More looks. More whispers. The Napa High gym could have been a hive of bees for all the buzzing zipping along the seats. The sound swirled around the old building, off the curved metal roof, the purple benches, the scoreboard, and the huge picture of the Napa mascot: a lady pirate dressed all in violet. The buzzing stopped at the Napa side, which was so crowded, kids looked like they'd been squeezed in with a trash compactor. The Redwood side was pretty full, too, especially considering the Grizzlies had endured a forty-five minute bus ride to get there. But now that they were in Napa, the Redwood fans were beginning to panic.

The horns sounded. Whitney and Jason and the rest of the cheerleaders cleared the floor, and the five starting players went out to half court for the opening tip-off. Except for Nick, who kept looking up at Tim sitting in the bleachers, the other players were trying to act like nothing was strange. But the fans realized with horror that what they'd feared was true — Tim Holt was not playing in the game.

"How does he look?" Celia asked Meg and Allie while she kept her eyes glued to the court. She couldn't bear to see Tim sitting up there instead of down on the floor with the other players, scrambling for the ball.

"Terrible," Meg replied. She could barely look herself, and she put a hand on Celia's arm to steady herself as much as her friend. She wondered how many Redwood kids knew what was really going on. She'd told Celia and Allie — and she would have told Sean, if he'd been on the bus with them — but Sean had gotten a ride, and now he sat up top, also alone, on the other side of the bleachers from Tim.

No one was taking this well, Celia thought. Besides all the staring and pointing, gossip was starting to break out. Natalie Bonwit, one of Whitney's crowd, was close enough so they could hear every word she was saying, and what Natalie was saying stung Celia, deep, deep inside. . . . Tim was stupid, he was flunking every single class. . . . Tim was freaking out, he couldn't take the pressure. . . . Tim was betraying every single kid at Redwood, and if they lost the game, and the championship, it would all be Tim's fault.

Trying to keep her feelings hidden, Celia held on to Meg and Allie and stole split second, painful glances at Tim, who looked as lonely and as sad as any person she had ever seen. The space between him and the rest of the Grizzlies reminded her of that poem she'd once read in English. No man is an island. But Tim *was* an island, at least the way he was sitting all alone up there now. But she didn't have time to think about it long. Allie was gripping her shoulder and yelling.

"Oh, no!"

Celia looked back down to the basketball court and saw a terrible commotion. A foul had been called against Gus Baldwin, and he was throwing his arms up in disgust. Nick calmed him, but by the time the incident was over, Napa had pulled ahead by five points. On the Napa side of the gymnasium the crowd was roaring.

"We're getting behind already," Allie whimpered.

Celia noticed that Meg was staring straight ahead at Jason, who was trying to combat the glum mood by doing one of his patented sideline cartwheels. It got a few claps but not many, and even when the band broke into the fight song, there seemed something droopy about their playing. The Grizzlies were definitely down. Ten minutes later they were almost out, and the droopiness on the Redwood side had turned to sullenness and anger. The whole season was going down the drain. The team was behind by nine points and no matter what they did or how hard they tried, Napa had the answer.

Meanwhile, the looks directed at Tim had grown more intense. Jason, for one, had started to seethe. He was directing his anger about the game totally at Tim, and he was whispering to other cheerleaders and band members, who got together to sneer and point. It made Celia shrink.

The horn blared for halftime, and the whole Napa side was on its feet, waving purple pennants and chanting, "PURPLE POWER, PURPLE POWER," rocking the gym with their happy voices. Jason came out in his red and blue and put two fingers in his ears, but he seemed to be showing more annoyance than guts or spirit. Then, instead of leading a cheer, he stood with his hands on his hips and glared blatantly up at Tim, who still sat all alone, the island of a man in the back row.

Whitney joined Jason — Celia figured that the common enemy had brought them together — and put her blue-gloved hand on his shoulder. One by one the other cheerleaders and yell leaders joined them, until, with the Napa side still screaming their heads off, twelve Grizzly cheerleaders stood like a jury, staring up at Tim, and pronouncing him guilty with their eyes. Tim leaned back, his cheek against the wall, as if he wanted to fade into the concrete and disappear. Suddenly, Celia was on her feet. Meg reached up to take her hand, "Cici, where are you. . . ."

It was too late. Celia was on her way. She stepped over three people and was clambering over to the aisle. But what was she going to do? Not another confrontation with Whitney. That would be a total disaster in front of everybody. Besides, that was just what she wanted to get away from. She was beginning to realize how stupid it was of her to give Whitney that much attention. Celia had isolated herself from so much at Redwood because she was afraid of what Whitney and other unimportant people thought of her. And looking at Tim on that top bench, she knew that she was doing the same dumb thing.

Celia climbed the bleachers. Past sweaters, books, purses; she walked over them or pushed them aside. Almost at the top, she grazed some man's hand and murmured a semicoherent apology as she ran up the last few empty bleachers, doing stag leaps from bench to bench. Finally she was there and, without hesitation, she plunked herself down next to Tim.

"Hi."

"Hi."

No words after that. Just a chilly, awkward quiet. Celia withered inside and swallowed hard.

194

This wasn't easy. Tim looked like he was about as glad she'd come up to sit with him as he would have been if she were radioactive. It was lonely, too, especially since people were still staring and pointing and whispering. The nearest person was twenty feet off, so far that Celia felt like she and Tim were in another county.

Tim leaned forward again, over his knees with hands folded, head down. Celia knew now that he was too humiliated to look at her. Maybe he still felt something for her, maybe he didn't, but as she sat up on that top bleacher, staring back at Whitney and the others, she realized that what she was about to do was as much for herself as it was for Tim.

"GO GRIZZLIES!!!" she shouted, hands cupped over her mouth.

Even above the Napa noise she could be heard, but not a single person responded. Now Celia stood up. If they wanted to stare, she'd give them something to stare at all right. She flashed back on her freshman stint as a cheerleader, remembering how to start a cheer and get the crowd going. "Give me a G!" she screamed, praying that the crowd would follow her.

No response.

She took a deep breath and yelled even louder. "GIVE ME AN R!" She waited and this time there was a tiny echo. Meg and Allie were the only ones to answer her.

Celia prayed and gave it all she had with another holler that tore at her throat. "GIVE ME AN I!" This time she heard another voice join her lead. Out of the corner of her eye she saw

Sean's red head crossing the top bleacher and moving closer. A second later he was standing next to her, hands cupped over his mouth, shouting, too.

"GIVE ME A Z — Z!" they both yelled at their loudest.

More people were looking up at them, nudging each other with elbows, smiling. "ZEE ZEE!" a few of them finally answered, then laughed.

Sean and Celia wouldn't let them go. "GIVE ME AN L!!!" Allie and Meg had climbed up next to them and were yelling, too. This time the response sent a thrill into Celia, it was so loud and full. "ELLLLLLLL!!!!"

The cheerleaders were starting to look around, conferring with each other at this rebellion in the crowd. Two of the girls took tentative positions, forming the "L"s with their bodies that they usually did on this cheer.

Maria Martinez, the Swain Twins, Nancy Carlin, Sam Pond, and others were climbing up and sitting down around Tim. His island was stretching, filling out, beginning to touch land on all sides.

"GIVE ME AN I!"

"I!" The voices were growing fuller, stronger.

"GIVE ME AN EEEEEEEEEEEEE!!!!"

"EEEEEEEEEEEEEEEEEEEE!!!!!"

Now all the cheerleaders were on the court, reluctantly joining the cheer. Even Jason had his megaphone up and was pretending to lead it, as if it had been his idea all along.

"GIVE ME AN S," screamed Celia, her friends

screaming with her. "WHAT DOES THAT SPELL?"

"GRIZZLIES!!!"

"WHAT????"

"GRIZZLIES!!!!!!!"

"I CAN'T HEAR YOU!!!!"

"GGGGRRRRRRRRRRRROWL!!!!!!!!!!!!"

As the crowd's cheering reached its peak, Tim stood up and cheered, too. People were still staring back at him, but their faces had turned softer, much more friendly. "When you coming back, Holt?" someone shouted. A few others smiled and waved.

"We miss you, Tim!"

"Let's go Redwood!"

Then the teams were running back onto the court, and the crowd turned back to watch the second half.

The Grizzlies almost caught up. In the fourth quarter they were within two points, and bolstered by their fans, they played their hearts out. Even though they lost at the end, they'd given a performance that any school could be proud of. That was just the way Celia felt, too; proud, as the bleachers started to empty and people headed for the buses back to Redwood. She'd stood up to make her way down to the floor, when she felt a hand on her arm. She turned and looked at Tim. His touch was gentle, his hand warm, and his eyes had that sweet, dark glimmer again. "Celia."

"Yes."

"Do you have to take the bus home?"

Celia's heart kicked into high gear. Other than cheering together they hadn't really spoken during the second half. "I don't think so."

"I drove. Maybe I could take you."

He looked down at his feet, sliding aside a program and a score card. Celia felt equally shy, breathless, totally opposite from the way she used to feel around boys. "I guess Meg could tell the driver I got a ride."

"Could she?"

"Sure." She called down two rows, where Meg and Allie were pulling on their jackets. Sean was no longer with them. "You guys, I'm getting a ride with Tim. Tell Mr. Johnson. Okay?" Meg and Allie tried not to make their smiles too obvious and answered with an okay sign. Celia turned back to Tim. "They'll tell him. We can go."

She felt so formal, like she was talking to someone she'd never met before. Silently she climbed down the bleachers. Kids stopped Tim on the way, asking him why he wasn't playing — which he answered honestly — telling him they hoped he was back on the team soon. But when Celia stepped down on the floor to wait for him, she got a jolt that made her budding good feelings evaporate. Whitney was waiting for her.

Christopher stood behind Whitney in a red parka, holding her pom-poms. His skiing tan was even darker than before, and he gave Celia an amused, conceited smile. Whitney walked right up to Celia, her condescension so strong it glowed on her porcelain cheeks. "What did I always say about you, Cavenaugh?"

198

"What?" Celia asked.

"I guess if you can't get a decent guy, then you just bring any guy who goes out with you down to your level."

"Oh?"

Whitney tossed back her fluffy hair and laughed. "It figures that the minute you start seeing Tim Holt, he turns into a pathetic zero."

Celia looked back up the bleachers. Tim was surrounded by about five kids, including two guys from the team, who'd run up to talk to him. She was glad that he hadn't heard Whitney. But amazingly, she wasn't that upset. Instead of getting boiling angry, she was actually feeling calmer. She found herself watching Whitney like she was a gross movie or a bug under a microscope — knowing that Whitney could say whatever she wanted, and it couldn't really hurt Celia at all. Celia could just study it, watch it go by, then draw her own conclusions. I don't have to stand up to Whitney or yell at her like I did freshman year, she thought. She was beyond that. She was a sophomore. All she had to do was walk away.

Celia turned her back on Whitney, waited for Tim, and quietly made her way out of the gym.

On the way home, Tim and Celia were anything but quiet. It was as if they'd been starved for conversation, and waiting for this ride to share every important thing in the world there ever was to say.

Celia talked and talked and talked. She told Tim about what happened freshman year with

Whitney and cheerleading; she told him about her parents' divorce and how her father was remarried in Texas and hardly ever visited her anymore. She told him about quitting her job at the mall and how she liked her new business class and might want to go further with it when she got to college. She told him about her old friends — how they were more like family to each other than mere friends — and how sometimes she wished that she'd been born to Nick's mom instead of her own because he had things so much easier.

In turn, Tim told her all about Jason and the cheating scheme. He talked about *his* parents' divorce; how he spent every summer in Los Angeles with his father, whether he liked it or not; how he wanted to be a coach when he grew up, and about this amazing kid in Cotter Valley named Billy Beacham, who was a crummy athlete but always got picked for the team because he could recite *Monty Python* routines and make them all laugh.

As they pulled up in front of her house, the rain had finally ended, and the street lamps glimmered down on sidewalks that looked washed and new. "He really knows all those *Monty Python* routines by heart?" Celia wondered.

"Not only that" — Tim laughed . . . a deep, honest laugh that Celia hadn't heard enough of — "but he can do all the different accents, too, and he's only eleven."

"That's unbelievable."

"You should come by and hear him sometime."

"You really want me to visit you in Cotter Valley again?"

Tim put his arm around her and pulled her in close. "Definitely."

Celia saw the lights in her living room flicker on and off twice. Her mom peeked out through the curtains and waved but didn't come out to say hello. Celia actually felt like it wouldn't have mattered if she did.

"It's funny," Tim told her. "I didn't play tonight; my team lost; we're no longer in first place, and I think it's been a terrific evening." They both looked out the windshield at the planters on Meg's porch and the big Redwood tree and the crescent moon.

The pressure of Tim's arm over Celia's shoulder warmed her whole body, even though it was cold enough to see little puffs every time they breathed. "I know what you mean," Celia agreed, snuggling even closer. "I know what you mean."

CHAPTER 19

For the next couple of weeks, the five friends didn't see much of each other.

Nick was busier than ever with basketball, Celia was preoccupied with a project for her business class and, of course, Tim. Meg had been recruited for girls' track by Miss Snyder and was spending every day after school running wind sprints. Sean was up to something, although nobody was quite sure exactly what it was.

Allie couldn't help thinking about Sean as she sat in front of the video monitor that displayed her "Nerds of the Future Make Friends with the Dinosaurs." It sat between two other video art projects in the converted farmhouse — one showing a flowing river with fish scuttling through, the other an abstract collection of bouncing circles and lines. Allie proudly believed that of the three, hers was the best.

The video projects stood in the middle of about forty other art pieces. All kinds of things were represented, everything from charcoal sketches and tissue paper collage to oil paintings and sculptures made of quilted fabric. Almost every inch of the old farmhouse was filled with some kind of display, leaving barely enough room for the viewers.

"Boy, this place sure has changed," Allie heard from the other side of the room. She spun around so quickly that her long earrings whisked her cheeks, and her bowler hat flopped onto the floor. It was L.P.

He was standing a few feet away, between a row of easels and a table of pottery. As he came toward her he did a double take at a life-sized figure made entirely of tin cans. His camera was around his neck, and he was peering around the way he did when he was taking pictures.

Allie picked her hat up off the floor, then nervously chewed her fingernail. She'd seen L.P. at school since their break up, but it had always been awkward. L.P. would say hello, she'd say hello back, and then they slid away from each other like two ice cubes. At first that had driven Allie into fits of despair — how could they act so unnatural? But after a week or two, she'd decided to look at it as kind of a challenge. She knew she was still in love with L.P., so she pretended everything was okay and this was simply a kind of "tough guy" game they were playing. . . . Who could be the iciest. That had helped her get through it, and in the last week or so she'd been so involved in her project that she hadn't thought about L.P. nearly as much. But that was last week and this was now, and Allie wasn't sure how much longer she could keep playing this absurd game.

"Hi," Allie said coolly.

L.P. had noticed her and was frantically pretending now that he was looking at the old building. The porch had been demolished, and the walls, which had been wood-paneled like a hunting lodge, were plastered over in a smooth white. The stairway had a banister, and there was even a sprinkler system in the ceiling. The only thing that remained of the farmhouse's old days was the mounted moose head hanging on the back wall. L.P. pointed to it. "At least he's still around."

Allie wasn't about to be distracted. "What are you doing here?" she asked, as if she had the upper hand. L.P. was acting like he'd only come to see the building, and her project was totally unimportant. Well, if he was going to be that way, then she was going to be just as tough.

He gestured to his camera. "I joined the newspaper staff last week. I'm covering the exhibit for an article."

Allie didn't say anything and after staring at her a second, L.P. took a deep breath and went on. "I have two photographs over there. Did you see them?" He pointed to the other side of the room.

Allie placed her hands on her soft hips, her anger growing. As if all she had to do was follow L.P.'s photographic career! Actually, she'd been so busy helping Mr. Thorson cart the monitors over and hook them up, she hadn't noticed that L.P.'s work was on display, too. "Believe it or not," she said in her most blasé tone, "I've had other things to think about." She turned away, searching the crowd for Celia or Meg, who were supposed to meet her there at four.

L.P. looked at her with those sweet, familiar brown eyes, as if he wasn't sure what he'd said wrong. He took a few steps toward her until he was quite close, stared at her face, and then winced. Allie felt her armor crumble. Maybe the game was over. Maybe he wanted to talk. One thing she knew for sure, all the good memories were coming back. The first time they'd met in this very room . . . the picnics and raft trips and museum outings they'd shared over the summer . . . the late nights sitting and talking in the apple orchard beside her house. The memories crept back, and she tried to make them go away, but they wouldn't disappear. Still, at least she'd learned something in these past two weeks. She didn't have to be with L.P. in order to feel like life had some purpose. She could do things on her own.

"I didn't mean that all you have to think about is my pictures, Al," L.P. volunteered, almost reading Allie's mind. That was another thing she remembered he could do. L.P. cleared his throat. "So, do you like the exhibit? Have you seen everything?"

She faced him and folded her arms. "In case you haven't noticed, I happen to have something on display here, too."

His eyes widened with interest, and he ran his hand through his hair in that way that always made it stand up. "Really? What?"

She mutely pointed at her video screen, too exasperated to speak.

L.P. stepped in front of it. He watched for a while, then slipped on his glasses and watched some more. Allie suddenly felt something she could only identify as stage fright. It was taking him forever to say anything. He was probably finding all kinds of things to be critical about.

But when he turned around he was chuckling. "Allie, it's great. It's funny, it's original. It's you!"

Allie couldn't keep the corners of her mouth from curling up, although she tried to keep up her guard. "Thanks. I guess."

"So Sean decided to work on it again?"

"For your information, Sean hasn't worked on this since the very beginning, and most of the stuff he did I had to redo anyway, and if you don't believe that I really did it, you can ask Mr. Thorson!"

Instead of being offended by her huffy tone, L.P. seemed even more impressed. He stared back at the screen, rubbing his hand across his hair, laughing some more, and pointing at the images. "Al, it's so good. You did this all by yourself? It's great."

"Gee, thanks," she responded curtly.

He frowned. "I mean it, Al. It's terrific. Why are you so mad?"

"Why are you so surprised? It's like you didn't think I could ever do anything on my own. Like I'm a baby or something." She lowered her voice as a set of parents came closer to look at the video screens.

"I never thought that," L.P. argued. "I always thought you could do anything you wanted. It was you who acted like you couldn't ever do anything on your own."

"I did not."

"You did, too."

Suddenly there were too many people milling around to continue arguing, so Allie just stood there, her hands in the pockets of her oversized vest, trying to look as mad as she could. It turned into a stare-down until she broke, and a goofy smile appeared on her face.

L.P. was smiling, too. He tentatively took one of her hands. "Oh, Al, I miss you."

"You do?"

He nodded.

"I guess I miss you, too," she finally admitted.

"Can't we get together and figure this out?" He pulled her into the corner away from the growing crowd. They were squeezed between a hanging mobile and a miniature model of a dinner party. "I never really wanted to break up. Did you?"

"I guess not."

"So let's go someplace and talk this over." He was already pulling her hands, teasing. "Come on. Right now. Let's go sit under the apple trees by your house."

Allie pulled back, laughing and shaking her head. She just missed crashing into a clay bust that looked like Cindy Furmin, a girl in her lit. class. "I can't."

"Why not?"

"It's too cold."

"I'll keep you warm."

Allie giggled; it was that old, loud, goofy giggle, and if she wasn't careful, everybody at the exhibit would soon be staring at her. "No," she said more seriously, "I have to stay here. I'm on duty watching the video monitors, making sure they keep working right."

"How about after that?"

"After that Meg and Celia are meeting me, and we're going downtown."

L.P. rolled his eyes. "Okay. How about after that?"

She twisted her hands away and started walking back to her project. "After that I guess you can call me," she said over her shoulder.

"Is that a promise?" he said, raising his camera.

"Maybe."

He snapped her picture. "It'd better be. I have it on film."

Allie laughed louder as he tripped over the tin can man and stumbled his way across the room.

When the three girls met later and started walking downtown, they marched in step along the sidewalk. Allie said it was like the *Wizard of Oz*, but Celia said it was like some commercial she'd seen for a life insurance company. Meg said she simply thought it was fun.

The rain was over, the fog had fled, but it was cold. Freakish for Northern California, but bone-chilling, teeth-chattering cold nonetheless. It made their march go pretty fast.

"Anyway," Celia said, blowing on her hands, "Tim's allowed to practice with the team again now. If he passes his test next week, he'll be able to play in the last two games, so maybe we'll still make the playoffs."

"Does he think he'll pass?" Meg asked, starting to jog in doubletime to keep warm.

"He's not sure, but he really understands it better than he did before."

"Well, Sean's been helping him," added Allie.

They stopped to wait for the light, all stamping the ground and rubbing their hands and watching their breath turn frosty and white.

"So do you think you and L.P. will really get back together?" Celia asked, bumping Allie with her shoulder.

Allie gave one of her supremely goofy faces and giggled. "We'll see. But I'd say there's a definite good chance."

That caused all three girls to hop up and down, hoot and clap. They were still hopping and whooping when a mint-green VW Rabbit pulled up alongside them and a very handsome, golden-haired boy stuck out his head.

"What are you guys doing, trying to get arrested or something?"

They all turned to look at the same time.

"NICK!" exclaimed Celia and Allie.

Meg stopped hopping and shivering and stood very still.

"Where are you going?" Nick asked.

"Downtown," Celia said, meeting him at the window. Allie quickly joined her. Meg didn't budge.

"Don't go down there," he wooed. He was wearing a Redwood High sweat shirt with a towel around his neck. "I'm on my way to get Sean. We're going over to Bayside to look at stereos. Come with us."

Celia and Allie both groaned.

"Borrring."

"Have you ever been with Sean in a stereo store? He has to look at everything for about five hours."

Nick leaned on the window frame and looked up at the darkening sky. "Come on. If you keep walking, you'll get frostbite, and then you'll get gangrene. And you know what happens when you get gangrene?"

"What?" Allie asked wide-eyed.

Nick put a hand to his face. "I don't want to tell you, it's too gross."

Allie slapped his arm. "Nick!"

"So you'd better just get in," Nick reasoned. "I promise we won't stay longer than half an hour."

Allie looked to Celia, who shrugged and smiled, so she opened the door. Neither girl noticed the strain on Meg's face or how she had suddenly gotten so quiet or the way she rushed past them to make sure she got in the backseat, so she wouldn't be next to Nick.

"It sure is a lot warmer in here," Allie remarked happily. She sat in the front and waved her hands at the heater. "So where are we going?" she asked, when Nick made a left turn, heading away from the center of Redwood Hills. The only things out this way were some industrial parks and the campus of Redwood College. "Where is Sean? I never see him after school anymore."

Nick drove steadily, only glimpsing up a few times to catch Meg in his mirror. "He's taking some special class at the college. He wouldn't tell me too much about it — he didn't even tell me he was doing it until a few days ago. I guess Thorson got him into it. Anyway, he really likes it."

"So that's where he's been," Allie said. "You think he might tell us. If he doesn't come see my video project, I'll never speak to him again."

"Don't worry, Al," Nick soothed, "he and I are going tomorrow."

"Good." Satisfied, Allie sat back, and they all watched the scenery as Nick pulled onto the college campus. Even though Allie's father taught here, it was still a scary, intimidating place. Nick pulled into the first parking lot, and they all looked out at the college students walking by.

"There he is!" Allie squealed, spotting Sean at the other end of an enormous lawn. "Let's surprise him." A second later, she and Celia hopped out of the car and were racing across the grass.

Left alone, Meg and Nick sat so quietly she could almost make out the conversation of two students at the other end of the parking lot. She leaned into the seat and stared out at the trees and bike paths and rectangular brick buildings. Finally Nick turned back to face her. Their eyes locked, and for a minute everything inside Meg went upside down.

"Hi," she whispered. She couldn't think of a single other thing to say.

"Hi." Nick drummed the back of the seat with his fingers. He was clearly as uncomfortable as she, which was weird considering that Nick was rarely uncomfortable, especially with her. "I heard you're not seeing Sandy anymore."

"Nope."

He heaved a loud sigh. "I'm sorry I was kind of a jerk, but you'll have to admit he's not the world's greatest guy."

"I know."

Nick drummed some more, and Meg stared out the window again. She found herself thinking about only one thing . . . Nick kissing her. She wondered if he was thinking about that, too. But she would never know, because she was certain that neither of them would ever mention it. In some ways it seemed to her like it had never happened and in others it seemed like it had happened a hundred times before. Finally she met Nick's eyes again and caught a glimpse of the same confusion that was in her own heart. She smiled sadly. He smiled back.

Then there was a loud knocking on the window, and Sean was pressing his face against the glass, while Allie beat on the hood, and Celia yelled, "Let us in! Let us in!"

Meg was grateful for the distraction and leaned forward to open the door. Allie and Sean tumbled into the backseat, both pink-cheeked from the cold and in high spirits. Celia quickly followed.

"You guys are so embarrassing." Sean laughed, his red hair falling over his forehead. He was wearing a sweater vest and a sportcoat, as if he was trying to look older. "I'm trying to create some kind of an image here for these college girls, and you come and blow it for me, just like that."

Even Meg had to laugh. She noticed that Nick seemed more relaxed, too, as he started the car and looked back at Sean. There was something about the five of them together that could sometimes make the world make sense.

"Let's go get something to eat," Celia suggested, leaning so far over the seat she almost fell into Sean's lap.

"How about the Chili Place?" Sean answered in retaliation. There were groans, tongues stuck out, and finally, giggles.

"Hey, c'mon you guys," Nick instructed. "We're sophomores. We're supposed to show a little class now."

"Where're we going, then?" Meg demanded, pressing herself closer to the back of Nick's seat.

"Yeah, what's your cool idea?" Allie challenged.

"Well," Nick fumbled, "I thought we might all share a nice comfortable meal at the . . . um . . . uh . . . well, heck, I know this place at the mall called the Chili Place and it's real close and. . . ."

Four pairs of arms reached out and began slapping and pinching and tickling Nick as he started yelling and laughing, and bumped the horn on his car.

Have you seen
NANCY DREW
lately?

Nancy Drew has become a girl of the 80s! There is hardly a girl from seven to seventeen who doesn't know her name.

Now you can continue to enjoy Nancy Drew in a new series, written for older readers – THE NANCY DREW FILES. Each book has more romance, fashion, mystery and adventure.

In THE NANCY DREW FILES, Nancy pursues one thrilling adventure after another. With her boundless energy and intelligence, Nancy finds herself enrolling at a crime-ridden high school, attending rock concerts and locating the missing star, skiing in Vermont with friends Bess and George and faithful boyfriend Ned, and temping at a teenage magazine based in wildly exciting New York.

COMING IN SPRING 1988

The Nancy Drew Files

No. 1 Secrets Can Kill
No. 2 Deadly Intent
No. 3 Murder on Ice
No. 4 Smile and Say Murder

ARMADA

STEVIE DAY SUPERSLEUTH
(that's me!)

I'm on my way to being the first female Commissioner of the Metropolitan Police. It's true I have a few personal problems: for a start I'm small and skinny and people are always mistaking me for a boy. I'm 14 – though you wouldn't think so – and my younger sister, Carla, not only looks older than me but she's much prettier too. Not that that really matters. You see, she doesn't have my brains.

If you want to see my razor-sharp mind in action or have proof of my brilliant powers of deduction then read about my triumphant successes in:

STEVIE DAY: Supersleuth
STEVIE DAY: Lonely Hearts
STEVIE DAY: Rat Race

Hairline Cracks
John Robert Taylor

Sam Lydney's mother knows too much. She has realized that a public inquiry into the safety of a local nuclear power station has been rigged and, despite his father's assurances, Sam is certain she's been kidnapped. He can trust no one except his resourceful friend Mo. They must work alone to piece together the clues and discover who has taken his mother and where she may be kept.

An Armada Original

On the Spot
Mark Daniel

Ben O'Connell has a problem. He is small. Humiliated at home and bullied at school, he seems a born loser. But Ben has a special talent for snooker and he's determined to reach the top.

It seems that no one can beat him and nothing will stand in his way – until scheming Perry Curling becomes his manager. To him, a boy like Ben is made for hustling round seedy snooker joints. Winning championships, says Curling, is the stuff dreams are made of. After all, this is tough '80s Merseyside.

But Ben is aiming for the top . . .

An Armada Original

Forthcoming teenage fiction
published in Armada

Class of 88 1–4
Linda A. Cooney

In A Spin
Mark Daniel

Nightmare Park
Linda Hoy

Sin Bin 1–4
Keith Miles

Run With the Hare
Linda Newbery

ARMADA